NIKOLÁY VASILÉVICH GÓGOL was born in 1809; his family were small gentry of Ukrainian cossack extraction, and his father was the author of a number of plays based on Ukrainian popular tales. He attended school in Nézhin and gained a reputation for his theatrical abilities. He went to St Petersburg in 1829 and with the help of a friend gained a post in one of the government ministries. Gógol was introduced to Zhukovsky, the romantic poet, and to Pushkin, and with the publication of *Evening on a Farm near Dikanka* (1831) he had an entrée to all the leading literary salons. He even managed for a short period to be Professor of History at the University of St Petersburg (1834–5). *Diary of a Madman* and *The Story of the Quarrel between Ivan Ivanovich and Ivan Nikiforovich* appeared in 1834, *The Nose* in 1836, and *The Overcoat* in 1842. Gógol also wrote the play *The Inspector* (1836), *Dead Souls* (1842), and several moralizing essays defending the Tsarist régime, to the horror of his liberal and radical friends. He lived a great deal abroad, mostly in Rome, and in his last years became increasingly prey to religious mania and despair. He made a pilgrimage to Jerusalem in 1848, but was bitterly disappointed in the lack of feeling that the journey kindled. He returned to Russia and fell under the influence of a spiritual director who told him to destroy his writings as they were sinful. He burned the second part of *Dead Souls*, and died in 1852 after subjecting himself to a severe régime of fasting.

RONALD WILKS was born in 1933. After training as a naval interpreter in Russian he went up to Trinity College, Cambridge. His translations include *The Little Demon* by Sologub (1962), and *My Childhood* by Gorky (1966, Penguin Classics); the second part of the Gorky trilogy, *My Apprenticeship*, will be appearing in the Penguin Classics shortly. Ronald Wilks is currently completing a thesis at London University.

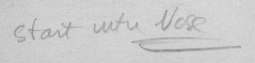

GOGOL

DIARY OF A MADMAN

AND OTHER STORIES

TRANSLATED WITH
AN INTRODUCTION BY
RONALD WILKS

PENGUIN BOOKS

Penguin Books Ltd, Harmondsworth, Middlesex, England
Penguin Books Inc., 7110 Ambassador Road, Baltimore, Maryland 21207, U.S.A.
Penguin Books Australia Ltd, Ringwood, Victoria, Australia

—

This translation first published 1972
Reprinted 1974

—

This translation copyright © Ronald Wilks, 1972

—

Made and printed in Great Britain by
Cox & Wyman Ltd, London, Reading and Fakenham
Set in Monotype Bembo

Contents

Introduction

IN the autumn of 1828 the nineteen-year-old Gogol wrote to a friend from his Ukrainian estate: 'When winter comes I'm going to St Petersburg without fail, and God knows where I'll end up after that. It's highly likely I'll go abroad and no one will hear a thing about me for years.' The following year, soon after his arrival in the Russian capital, he was already complaining to his mother: 'Petersburg is not half what I expected – I had thought of it as much more beautiful, magnificent, and it seems people have been spreading false rumours about it . . . It is an amazingly quiet place; the people there seem more dead than alive. All the civil servants and officials can talk about is their department or government office; everything seems to have been crushed under a great weight, everyone is drowned by the trivial, meaningless labours at which he spends his useless life.'

Hardly favourable impressions of the city which supplied the material and background for *Diary of a Madman* and two other stories in this selection. Gogol had left his native Ukraine with high hopes of a great literary career in St Petersburg. With him he had taken his first longish work, a very poor idyll written in the then fashionable sentimental German style, *Hans Kuchelgarten*. This he published at his own expense, under a pseudonym, but it was a complete failure, and Gogol collected and burned all the copies he could lay his hands on. Bitterly disappointed, he decided to escape from the capital (the first instance of his lifelong, incurable *Wanderlust*) and set sail for Lubeck, but after a few weeks his money ran out and he returned to the scene of his first failure. This time, however, a friend of the family pulled the necessary strings and Gogol entered one of the government ministries. But he had no wish to become one of those grovelling pen-pushers with their 'trivial, meaningless labours': his heart was set on a literary career.

With the help of more influential friends Gogol was soon taken under the wing of Zhukovsky, the great romantic poet of 'enchanting sweetness' as Pushkin called him, and not much time passed before Gogol was introduced to Pushkin himself. In his time off from office work Gogol had been preparing his first collection of stories, *Evenings on a Farm near Dikanka*, which met with immediate acclaim and from then onwards he had entrée to all the leading literary salons, which played a major part in the intellectual life of the time. The stories are the direct fruit of his life in the Ukraine, where he had lived since his birth and which he had now left for the great city.

Gogol's father was a small landowner with a talent for writing comedies in the traditional Ukrainian style. His mother, a highly devout and sensitive woman, doted on him and smothered him with affection and religious instruction. Gogol was a sickly, ugly child; at the local boarding school he was laughed at for his clumsiness and unprepossessing appearance, and nicknamed 'the mysterious dwarf'. He was particularly unpopular with his teachers, who constantly recorded his laziness, clownish behaviour and stubbornness. Gogol soon showed how he could retaliate against his tormentors by spiteful and deadly convincing mimicry. He began to gain a reputation for his imitations, and also for his theatrical ability, most probably inherited from his father. He had already written, chiefly for the school magazine, some short stories and poetry – of little value, in fact, but showing clear signs of a rapidly growing literary talent.

This was the life Gogol left behind when he went to St Petersburg to seek fame and fortune. The present selection of stories is set both in his native Ukraine and in St Petersburg,

8

that city which was to have such an obsessive effect on him and, later, on Dostoyevsky.

Towards the end of 1834 Gogol wrote ironically to Pushkin: '*Diary of a Madman* met with a rather unpleasant little snag from the Censor yesterday. But thank God things are a little better today. At least, all I have to do is throw out the *best parts*.'

Like *The Overcoat*, the *Diary*, set in St Petersburg, has as its 'hero' the totally insignificant downtrodden clerk engaged in a hopeless struggle with the rigid, highly impersonal State bureaucratic machine of Nicholas I's oppressive regime. The 'hero', a minor civil servant called Poprishchin, whose hair sticks out like hay, who is shabbily dressed and spends his time sharpening 'His Excellency's quill pens', has a position in the social scale which is quite fixed and immutable. Ludicrously for him, he is in love with the empty-headed daughter of 'His Excellency', but being an absolute nobody, he cannot possibly hope to compete with the fops and gentlemen of the court who grab 'all the good things in this world'. With the development of his madness he sees every door closed to him and gradually becomes convinced he is the rightful heir to the Spanish throne (the dispute over the Spanish succession was a subject of topical interest, as was the July revolution in France, and the *Diary* contains numerous references to these events). In the end he cuts up his civil service uniform and makes a 'Royal' mantle out of it, whereupon he is carted off to a lunatic asylum which he takes to be the Spanish Royal Palace.

When Gogol wrote this story he was very interested in the subject of madness. His censored play, *Vladimir Third Class*, dealt with this subject and his friend Annenkov recalls meetings at Gogol's flat where stories were told about madness and the development of *idées fixes* in case histories of lunatics. In the *Diary* Gogol portrays with an uncanny understanding the development of madness, with the madman finding completely logical (in *his* eyes) reasons for everything that happens to him. Even when Poprishchin is knocked around and beaten with a

9

stick in the asylum, he still thinks this is some sort of initiatory test for the future King of Spain. In a final moment of illumination the madman wishes to be borne aloft on the winged troika (a recurring symbol of escape with Gogol, later to appear in Dostoyevsky's *Brothers Karamazov*) to flee from the world of reality.

Here we find expressed the essential absurdity and tragedy of life, where dream and reality merge so that we have no means of distinguishing what is true from the illusory, what has value from what is worthless: this is Gogol's vision of the world, and in the *Diary* are voiced many of the author's own thwarted desires and obsessions. A Soviet critic has written: 'No other story of Gogol's is so packed with comedy as the *Diary of a Madman*, and yet this is a tragedy.'

The Nose was published in 1836, in Pushkin's *Contemporary*, after being turned down by the *Moscow Observer* as 'dirty and trivial'. Few stories have met with such a variety of interpretations as to its 'real' meaning. Some critics have approached it from the biographical point of view and seen it either as an expression of Gogol's fear of sexual relations (with the cutting off of the nose as a clear case of a castration complex) or as a reflection of a morbid sensitivity on the author's part about his own curiously elongated nose. Others have seen it as a wild, trivial fantasy, of no interest either for literary critic or psychoanalyst. Others regard it as a savage satire on St Petersburg and its stupid, pompous, vain and self-seeking civil service officials and its vast, hierarchical bureaucracy. However it may be interpreted, *The Nose* is a masterpiece of narrative comic art, with dream and reality intermingling to such an extent that it is hard to tell where the two divide.

Noses, snuff-taking and all the apparatus of sneezing appear constantly in Gogol's work. In addition, the literature of the time was full of jokes and stories about noses. Gogol was much influenced by Sterne, whose *Tristram Shandy* was published in a Russian translation in 1804–7; and some parts of *The Nose* distinctly recall Slawkenbergius's tale in that novel, with its mock-serious dissertation on noses. The digressive self-parodying style, the nebulous 'asides' where the author confesses that he himself is mystified as to what is going on, are all strongly reminiscent of Sterne.

The unfortunate character who suffers this disaster is a Major Kovalyov, a smug, ambitious ladies' man who wakes up one morning to find his nose has disappeared. It turns up inside a roll at a barber's breakfast table. In losing his nose, he is not only deprived of all status, but cannot visit his lady friends (here the symbolism of a *sexual* deprivation is obvious). The ensuing scene in the Cathedral, the visit to the Police Inspector, the newspaper office – all of these incidents give Gogol full scope for biting satire. Then, without any explanation at all (the essence of this story is that nothing *is* explained) the vagrant nose returns to its rightful owner.

As an indication of the idiocy of the censorship in Gogol's day, in the original version of the story the nose's visit to the Kazan Cathedral was objected to on religious grounds, and Gogol had to make the nose visit a shopping arcade instead. In a letter to Pogodin at the time he writes: 'If your stupid censors start quarrelling that a nose could not visit the Kazan Cathedral, then I might let it go to a Catholic Church instead. However, I can't believe they've taken leave of their senses to such an extent as this.'

The Overcoat is one of Gogol's finest works and one of the greatest short stories ever written. Published in 1842, it is set, like *The Nose* and the *Diary of a Madman*, in St Petersburg, that 'graveyard of dreams' as Gogol called it, Pushkin's vast fantastic impersonal city, which was so to obsess Dostoyevsky and later writers with its very intangibility, its insufferable summers, its mists, and its white nights. For Gogol the city is elusive, mysterious, and, above all, a place of utter alienation. The bewilderment aroused by the city is constantly voiced by Gogol in the mystifying technique of the Petersburg cycle, where seemingly concrete objects and events became shrouded in mist, where we are continually finding the qualifications 'God knows where or why' or 'I don't remember in *which* town' or 'perhaps it's better not to say in *which* department.' And further mystification is produced by Gogol's calling his very reportage into doubt.

In this highly rarefied atmosphere, in a city where the individual loses all identity, a poor clerk called Akaky Akakievich, a nonentity from the start, meets disaster and is carted away to be buried as though he had never even existed.

According to the memoirist Annenkov, Gogol took the subject of *The Overcoat* from an apparently true story about a government clerk, a passionate duck-shooter, who, after undergoing enormous sacrifices to buy himself a new rifle, loses it during his very first expedition, when it is knocked overboard. He becomes seriously ill and only survives because his friends get up a collection and buy him a new rifle. Akaky Akakievich is an insignificant civil service clerk whose sole delight in life is to copy out government documents one after the other, an absolutely mechanical operation but one which gives him enormous pleasure. Discovering that his overcoat has reached the final stages of disintegration and has become the laughing-stock of the whole office, after much hardship and self-sacrifice he manages to scrape enough money together to buy a new one. On his way home after a reception, given by his office friends partly to celebrate the new overcoat, he is stopped by some thieves in the middle of one of those vast, apparently endless squares in Petersburg and cruelly robbed. The shock brings on a high fever from which Akaky Akakievich dies, and he is then carted away to be buried. But he is not done with yet, and his ghost returns to search for the missing garment, attacking high-ranking officials at night and stripping them of their overcoats.

With its ostensibly strong humanitarian leaning, and its picture of a poor snivelling clerk being mocked and scorned,

The Overcoat was taken by contemporary critics (and later by the Soviets) as the fountainhead of the great school of 'social sympathy' in Russian literature. Dostoyevsky is recorded as saying: 'We have all come from under *The Overcoat*', and the great critic Belinsky read all kinds of humanitarian messages into it. But it is likely (if the story can be said to have any message) that in the hero's brief acquisition of status through the new overcoat, Gogol is simply telling us we should not pursue what is superficial and external to our true selves, what is mere show and pretence.

As the Symbolist critics at the turn of the century were the first to realize, *The Overcoat* is very much more than a story with a moral. The use of language alone (as opposed to any conscious effort on the author's part to impose his vision or message) to create what is literally another world, where logic does not apply, where values become transmuted and the world is turned upside down, is quite extraordinary. *The Overcoat* is written in a conversational style reminiscent of the old Russian *skaz*, or dramatic monologue (Gogol was a superb reader of his own works) and contains a strange mixture of language: now it is chatty and friendly, now ironical, now completely impersonal, now sentimental. And this strange medley is shot with witty anecdotes and startling asides which transfer the whole action to another plane of reality.

Gogol did not so much work from imagination (he once told Annenkov that an author could quite well write a successful story by describing a room with which he is *familiar*) as by using apparently irrelevant, trivial details to astonishing effect. Invariably these details are physical, but not at all in the sense in which Tolstoy uses them to develop his characters. Gogol's characters do not have psychological depth and are developed in the main purely by external physical descriptions. Rightly they have been called waxlike figures, mere puppets; apart from their physically described idiosyncrasies they have no reality, but are grotesque caricatures, a projection of

13

Gogol's imagination which so exaggerates the trivial that it is trivial no more.

In *The Overcoat* much of this extraordinary effect of bewilderment and illogicality is gained by the repeated and unusual use of simple words such as 'even'. (This word occurs over sixty times in the story.) To provide two examples: the frost attacks *even* high-ranking officials, as if such persons should be immune. Or, again, describing the clerk's humble origin, Gogol writes: 'His father, his grandfather, and *even* his brother-in-law and all the other Bashmachkins went around in boots' – as if there were some reason why his relatives should not be included in the category of boot-wearers. A further indication that this is not a normal world is given by the implication that when piglets rush out of private houses and knock over policemen this is in the natural order of things. In short, this story is a perfect example of Gogol's subjective art: without analysing reality or even criticizing it, he selects and rearranges his material so that in the end we have a grotesque world where nothing has value, where no logic applies, where all is illusion and deceit.

How Ivan Ivanovich quarrelled with Ivan Nikiforovich was first published in the almanac *Novoselye* (*House-warming*) in 1834, and is part of the group of stories set in his native Ukraine.

After hearing Gogol read it to him, Pushkin remarked: 'Very original and very funny', while Belinsky went into raptures over it. The story concerns two bosom friends living an idyllic, vegetable existence in a small Ukrainian village. Their peace and calm is forever broken when one of them, after an argument, calls the other a goose. There follow interminable lawsuits and an unsuccessful attempt on the part of the mayor and people of the village to reconcile the former friends. Years later, when the author returns to Mirgorod, the lawsuits are still pending. The Ukrainians were notorious for their endless lawsuits, and in 1825 V. Narezhny, a Ukrainian writer, had published a story entitled *The Two Ivans, or a*

Passion for Litigation, which was similar to Gogol's even though Narezhny's litigants were reconciled. As so often in Gogol, tragedy comes through the magnification and extension of the very trivial and banal and for this reason we have a vision of life as absurd and meaningless. The story ends on a dismal note, with the often-quoted closing line: 'It's a depressing world, gentlemen.'

For all this, the tale is full of delightful comic touches and some typically Gogolian descriptions, such as the humorous picture of Ivan Nikiforovich's clothes being hung up to air. Equally striking are the description of the village banquet with the carriage drawn up outside, the enumeration of Ukrainian national dishes, and the wicked parody of legal jargon in the plaints submitted to the Mirgorod court.

Ivan Fyodorovich Shponka and his Aunt belongs to the second part of the *Evenings on a Farm near Dikanka* series, which was set in the Ukraine and first established Gogol's reputation as a writer. One of Gogol's earlier works, it shows his genius for producing the extraordinary out of apparently insignificant details. Ivan Shponka is a shy, narrow-minded landowner of small intelligence but great application who, at his aunt's request, resigns his commission in the army to go and help her on the small estate. At school he was a model pupil. Later, he never joined his army friends in their wild drinking and gambling, preferring instead to stay in his quarters polishing buttons or setting mousetraps. After his return to the estate, he becomes a 'model' farmer, but is completely dominated by his very strong-minded aunt, whom everyone holds in awesome respect. At length his aunt decides it is time for him to get married. During a visit to a local estate, he is introduced to one of the landowner's two sisters, and when the two are left alone, all Ivan Shponka can find to talk about is the plague of flies that summer – in between long, very painful silences. Despite his aunt's exhortations, he resolutely refuses to get married, and in fact is horrified by the thought. At the end of the story he has a nightmare, dreaming that he is already married. In this nightmare, in which earlier elements from the story make their reappearance and are subtly interweaved, every object is transformed into a wife, and he sees wives everywhere, even in his hat. Gogol's own so-called 'sterility complex' and fear of sexual relations are possibly reflected here. It is interesting to note that Gogol generally portrays women either as delicate, ethereal, impossibly unattainable beauties, or as viragos or witches, in league with the devil and ready to lure man to destruction (as in the *Diary*). In *Shponka*, also, we see in prototype many of Gogol's best-known stylistic mannerisms, his well-contrived mock-serious descriptions (the account of the aunt's antediluvian carriage is a good example) and his love of comparing people to inanimate objects. Moreover, several major characters in later works, particularly *Dead Souls*, can be seen here in their formative stages. The closing sentence, where Gogol tells us the aunt is about to hatch a new plot, which 'we will hear about in the next chapter' is merely a joke played on the reader, in the tradition of Sterne: Gogol has no intention of continuing this story.

More than any other great nineteenth-century Russian writer Gogol presents very considerable difficulties for the translator. His prose is rhythmic, musical, high-pitched, running the whole gamut of literary style. In this collection I have tried to convey the unique 'flavour' of one of the most fascinating – and at the same time most elusive – of all the great writers of nineteenth-century Russia.

Diary of a Madman

October 3rd

SOMETHING very peculiar happened today. I got up rather late, and when Mavra brought my clean shoes in I asked her what the time was. When she told me it was long past ten I rushed to get dressed. To be honest with you, if I'd known the sour look I was going to get from the head of our department I wouldn't have gone to the office at all. For some time now he's been saying: 'Why are you always in such a muddle? Sometimes you rush around like a madman and make such a mess of your work, the devil himself couldn't sort it out. You start paragraphs with small letters and leave out the date and reference number altogether.' Damned old buzzard! Seeing me in the Director's office sharpening His Excellency's quills must have made him jealous. To cut a long story short, I'd never have gone to the office in the first place if there hadn't been a good chance of seeing the cashier and making the old Jew cough up a small advance somehow or other. What a man! The Last Judgement will be upon us before you can get a month's pay out of *him* in advance. Even if you're down to your last kopeck, you can go on asking until you're blue in the face, but that old devil won't give in. I've heard people say his own cook slaps him on the face in the flat. The whole world knows about it. I don't see there's any advantage working in our department. No perks at all. It's a different story in the Provincial Administration or in the Civil or Treasury Offices. You'll see someone sitting there curled up in a corner scribbling away. He'll be wearing a filthy old frock coat and just one look at his mug is enough to make you spit. But you should see the country house he rents! Just offer him a gilt china cup and all he'll say is: 'That's what you give a *doctor*!' He'll only be satisfied with a pair of racehorses, or a drozhky, or a beaver skin that cost three hundred roubles. To look at him you'd think he was so meek and mild, and he talks with such refinement: 'Please be so good as to lend me that little knife to sharpen my quills.' But just give him the chance and he'll strip any petitioner until there's only the shirt left on his back. I must admit, it's very civilized working in our department, everything's kept cleaner than you'll ever see in a Provincial Office. And we have mahogany tables, and all the Principals use the polite form of address. But really, if it weren't for the snob value, I'd have given in my notice long ago.

I put on my old overcoat and took my umbrella, as it was simply teeming down outside. There wasn't a soul about; all I could see were a few old peasant women sheltering under their skirts, some Russian merchants under their umbrellas and one or two messengers. As for better-class people, there weren't any, except for a civil servant. I spotted him at the crossroads. As soon as I saw him I said to myself: 'Aha, you're not going to the office, my friend, you're after that girl dashing along over there – and having a good look at her legs into the bargain.' What beasts our civil servants are! Good God, they'd leave any officer standing and get their claws into anything that goes past in a bonnet. While I was engrossed with these thoughts, a carriage drew up in front of a shop I happened to be passing. I saw at once this was our Director's. He couldn't be wanting anything in there, so he must have called for his daughter, I thought. I flattened myself against the wall. A footman opened the carriage door and out she fluttered, just like a little bird. The way she looked first to the right, then to the left, her eyes and her eyebrows flashing past . . . God in heaven, I thought, I'm lost, lost forever! Strange *she* should venture out in all that rain! Now just you try and tell me women aren't mad on clothes. She didn't recognize me, and I tried to muffle myself up as best I could, because my overcoat, besides being covered all over in stains, had gone out of fashion ages ago. Nowadays

18

they're all wearing coats with long collars, but mine were short, one over the other. And you couldn't really say the cloth had been waterproofed.

Her little dog wasn't quite quick enough to nip in after her and had to stay out in the street. I'd seen that dog before. She's called Medji. I hadn't been there more than a minute when I heard a faint little voice: 'Hello, Medji!' Well, I never! Who was that talking? I looked around and saw two ladies walking along under an umbrella: one was old, but her companion was quite young. They'd already gone past when I heard that voice again: 'Shame on you, Medji!' What was going on, for heaven's sake? Then I saw Medji sniffing round a little dog following the two ladies. 'Aha,' I said to myself, 'It can't be true, I must be drunk.' But I hardly ever drink. 'No Fidèle, I told myself, 'you're quite mistaken.' With my own eyes I actually saw Medji mouth these words: 'I've been, bow wow, very ill, bow wow.' Ah, you nasty little dog! I must confess I was staggered to hear it speak just like a human being. But afterwards, when I'd time to think about it, my amazement wore off. In fact, several similar cases have already been reported. It's said that in England a fish swam to the surface and said two words in such a strange language the professors have been racking their brains for three years now to discover what it was, so far without success. What's more, I read somewhere in the papers about two cows going into a shop to ask for a pound of tea. Honestly, I was much more startled when I heard Medji say: 'I *did* write to you, Fidèle. Polkan couldn't have delivered my letter.' I'd stake a month's salary that that was what the dog said. Never in my life have I heard of a dog that could write. Only noblemen know how to write correctly. Of course, you'll always find some traders or shopkeepers, even serfs, who can scribble away: but they write like machines – no commas or full stops, and simply no idea of style.

I was really astonished at all this. To be frank, quite recently I've started hearing and seeing things I'd never heard or seen before. So I said to myself, 'I'd better follow this dog and find out who she is and what she's thinking about.' I unrolled my umbrella and followed the two ladies. We crossed Gorokhovaya Street, turned into Meshchanskaya Street, then Stolyanaya Street, until we got to Kokushkin Bridge and stopped in front of a large house. 'I know this house,' I said to myself; 'it's Zverkov's.' What a dump! Everybody seems to live there: crowds of cooks, foreigners, civil servants. They live just like dogs, all on top of each other. A friend of mine who plays the trumpet very well lives there. The ladies went up to the fifth floor. 'Fine,' I thought. 'I shan't go in now, but I'll make a note of the address and come back as soon as I have a moment to spare.'

October 4th

Today is Wednesday, and that's why I went to see the head of our department in his office. I made sure I got there early and sat down to sharpen all the quills.

Our Director must be a very clever man: his study is full of shelves crammed with books. I read some of their titles: such erudition, such scholarship! Quite above the head of any ordinary civil servant. All in French or German. And you should look into his face, and see the deep seriousness that gleams in his eyes! I have yet to hear him use *one* more word than is necessary. He might perhaps ask as you handed him some papers: 'What's the weather like?' And you would reply, 'Damp today, Your Excellency.' No, you can't compare him with your ordinary clerk. He's a true statesman. May I say, however, that he has a special fondness for me. If only his daughter . . . scum that I am! Never mind, better say nothing about that. I've been reading the *Little Bee*.* A crazy lot, those

* Gogol is referring to the Petersburg journal *The Northern Bee*, which enjoyed police protection and vilely attacked the great writers and critics of the day – Pushkin, Gogol, Belinsky, Lermontov. Its founder, Bulgarin, in the pay of the police, was called 'the reptile journalist'. (Trans.)

French! What *do* they want? My God, I'd like to give them all a good flogging. There was a very good account of a ball written by a landowner from Kursk. They certainly know how to write, those landowners from Kursk! At that moment I noticed it was already past 12.30 and that our Director hadn't left his bedroom. But about 2.30 something happened that no pen could adequately describe. The door opened. I thought it was the Director and leapt up from my chair, clutching my papers: but it was her, herself in person! Holy Fathers, how she was dressed! Her dress was white, like a swan. What magnificence! And when she looked at me it was like the sun shining, I swear it! She nodded and said: 'Has papa been here?' Oh what a voice! A canary, just like a canary! I felt like saying to her: 'Your Excellency, don't have me put to death, but if that is your wish, then let it be by your own noble hand.' But I was almost struck dumb, blast it, and all I could mumble was 'No, Miss.' She looked at me, then at the books, and dropped her handkerchief. I threw myself at it, slipped on the damned parquet floor and nearly broke my nose. I regained my balance however, and picked up the handkerchief. Heavens, what a handkerchief! Such a fine lawn, and smelling just like pure ambergris.

You could tell from the smell it belonged to a general's daughter. She thanked me, and came so near to smiling that her sweet lips almost parted, and with that she left. I worked on for about another hour until a footman suddenly appeared with the message: 'You can go home now, Axenty Ivanovich, the master's already left the house.' I can't stand that brood of flunkeys: they're always sprawled out in the hall and it's as much as you can do to get one little nod of acknowledgement from them. What's more, one of those pigs once offered me some snuff – without even getting up. Don't you know, ignorant peasant, that I am a civil servant and of noble birth? All the same, I picked up my hat, put my coat on *myself* – because those fine gentlemen wouldn't dream of helping you –

and left the office. For a long time I lay on my bed at home. Then I copied out some very fine poetry:

> An hour without seeing you
> Is like a whole year gone by
> How wretched my life's become
> Without you I'll only fret and sigh.

Must be something by Pushkin. In the evening I wrapped myself up in my overcoat and went to Her Excellency's house, and waited a long time outside the entrance just to see her get into her carriage once more. But no, she didn't come out.

November 6th

The head of the department was in a terrible mood. When I got to the office he called me in and took this line with me: 'Will you please tell me what your game is.' 'Why, nothing,' I answered. 'Are you sure? Think hard! You're past forty now, and it's time you had a bit more sense. Who do you think you are? Do you imagine I haven't heard about your tricks? I know you've been running after the Director's daughter! Take a good look at yourself. *What* are you? Just nothing, an absolute *nobody*. You haven't a kopeck to bless yourself with. Just take a look in the mirror – fancy *you* having thoughts about the General's daughter!' To hell with it, his own face puts you in mind of those large bottles you see in chemists' windows, what with that tuft of hair he puts in curlers. And the way he holds his head up and smothers his hair in pomade! Thinks he can get away with anything! Now I can understand why he's got it in for me: seeing me get some preferential treatment in the office has made him jealous. I don't care a hoot about him! Just because he's a court councillor he thinks he's Lord God Almighty! He lets his gold watch chain dangle outside his waistcoat and pays thirty roubles for a pair of shoes. He can go to hell! Does he think I'm the son of a commoner, or tailor, or

22

a non-commissioned officer? I'm a gentleman! I could get promotion if I wanted! I'm only forty-two, that's an age nowadays when one's career is only just beginning. Just you wait, my friend, until I'm a colonel, or even something higher, God willing. I'll get more respect than *you*. Where did you get the idea *you're* the only person whom we're supposed to look up to around here? Just give me a coat from Ruch's,* cut in the latest style; I'll knot my tie like you do: and then you won't be fit to clean my boots. It's only that I'm short of money.

November 8th

I went to the theatre today. The play was about the Russian fool, Filatka. I couldn't stop laughing. They also put on some sort of vaudeville with some amusing little satirical poems about lawyers, and one Collegiate Registrar in particular. So near the knuckle, I wonder they got past the censor. As for merchants, the author says straight out that they're swindling everyone and that their sons lead a dissolute life and have thoughts of becoming members of the aristocracy. There was a very witty couplet about the critics, saying they do nothing but pull everything to pieces, so the author asks for the audience's protection. A lot of very amusing plays are being written these days. I love going to the theatre. As long as I've a kopeck in my pocket you can't stop me. But these civil servants of ours are such ignorant pigs, you'd never catch *those* peasants going, even if you gave them a ticket for nothing. One of the actresses sang very well. She reminded me of . . . ah! I'm a shocker! . . . Silence! The less said the better!

November 9th

At eight o'clock I set off for the office. The head of the department pretended he hadn't seen me come in. I played the same

*Ruch – a famous tailor of the day. (Trans.)

game, just as if we were complete strangers. Then I started checking and sorting out some documents. At four o'clock I left. I passed the Director's flat, but there didn't seem to be anybody in. After dinner I lay on my bed most of the evening.

November 11th

Today I sat in the Director's office and sharpened twenty-three quills for him – and for *her*. Ah, four quills for Her Excellency! He loves having a lot of pens around the place. Really, he must have a very fine brain! He doesn't say very much, but you can sense his mind is working the whole time. I'd like to know what he's hatching in that head of his. And those people with all their puns and court jokes – I wish I knew more about them and what goes on at that level of society.

Often I've thought of having a good talk with His Excellency, but somehow I'm always stuck for words: I begin by saying it's cold or warm outside, and that's as far as I get. I'd like to have a peep into the drawing-room but all I ever manage to see is another door which is sometimes open, and leads off to another room. Ah, what luxury! The china and mirrors! I'd love to see that part of the house where Her Excellency . . . yes, that's what I'd dearly love to see, her boudoir, with all those jars and little phials, and such flowers, you daren't even breathe on them. To see her dress lying there, more like air than a dress. And just one peep in her bedroom to see what wonders lie there, sheer paradise, more blissful than heaven. One glance at that little stool where she puts her tiny foot when she steps out of bed. And then, over that tiny foot, she starts pulling on her snowy white stocking. Ah, never mind, never mind, enough said . . .

Today something suddenly dawned on me which made everything clear: I recalled the conversation I'd heard between the two dogs on Nevsky Avenue. I thought to myself 'Good, now I'll find out what it's all about. Somehow I must get hold

24

of the letters that passed between those two filthy little dogs. There's sure to be something there.' To be frank, once I very nearly called Medji and said: 'Listen, Medji, we're alone now. If you want I'll shut the door so no one can see. Tell me everything you know about the young lady, who she is and what she's like. I swear I won't tell a soul.'

But that crafty dog put her tail between her legs, seemed to shrink to half her size, and went quietly out through the door, as though she had heard nothing. I'd suspected for a long time that dogs are cleverer than human beings. I was even convinced she could speak if she wanted to, but didn't, merely out of sheer cussedness. Dogs are extraordinarily shrewd, and notice everything, every step you take. No, whatever happens, I shall go to the Zverkovs tomorrow and cross-examine Fidèle, and with any luck I'll get my hands on all the letters Medji wrote to her.

November 12th

At two in the afternoon I set off with the firm intention of seeing Fidèle and cross-examining her. I can't stand the smell of cabbage; the shops along the Meshchanskaya just reek of it. What with this, and the infernal stench coming from under the front doors of all the houses, I held my nose and ran for all I was worth.

If that's not bad enough, those beastly tradesmen let so much soot and smoke pour out of their workshops that it's quite impossible for any respectable gentleman to take a stroll these days.

When I reached the sixth floor and rang the bell, a quite pretty-looking girl with tiny freckles came to the door. I recognized her as the same girl I'd seen walking with the old lady. She blushed slightly and straight away I realized that the little dear needed a boyfriend. 'What do you want?' she said. 'I must have a talk with your dog,' I replied. The girl was quite stupid – I could see that at once. While I was standing there the dog came out barking at me. I tried to catch hold of her but the nasty little bitch nearly sank her teeth into my nose. However, I spotted her basket in the corner. That's what I was after! I went over to it, rummaged around under the straw and to my great delight pulled out a small bundle of papers. Seeing this, that filthy dog first bit me on the thigh and then, when she'd sniffed around and discovered I'd taken the papers, started whining and pawing me, but I said to her: 'No, my dear, good-bye!' and took to my heels. The girl must have thought I was mad, as she seemed scared out of her wits.

When I arrived home, I intended starting work right away sorting the papers out, because I can't see all that well by candlelight. But Mavra decided the floor needed washing. Those stupid Finns always take it into their heads to have a good clean up at the most inconvenient times. So I decided to go for a walk and have a good think about what had happened earlier. Now at last I would find out every little detail of what had been going on, what was in their minds, who were the main actors in the drama, in fact, nothing would be hidden from me: those letters would tell me everything. 'Dogs are a clever species,' I told myself. 'They're well versed in diplomacy, and therefore everything will be written down, including a description of the Director and his private life. And there'll be something about *her*, but never mind that now . . . Silence!' I returned home towards the evening and spent most of the time lying on my bed.

November 13th

Well now, let's have a look: the letter is quite legible, though the handwriting looks a bit doggy. Let's see: 'Dear Fidèle, I still can't get used to your plebeian name. Couldn't they find a better one for you? Fidèle, like Rosa, is in very vulgar taste.

26

However, all that's neither here nor there. I am very glad we decided to write to each other.'

The letter is impeccably written. The punctuation is correct and even the letter 'ye' is in the right place. Even the head of our department can't put a letter together so well, for all his telling us that he went to some university or other. Let's see what else there is: 'I think that sharing thoughts, feelings and experiences with another person is one of the greatest blessings in this life.' Hm! He must have found that in some translation from the German. The name escapes me for the moment.

'I am speaking from experience, though I've never ventured further than our front door. Don't you think I lead a very agreeable life? My mistress, whom Papa calls Sophie, is passionately fond of me.'

Ah! Never mind! Silence!

'Papa often likes to fondle and stroke me as well. I take cream with my tea and coffee. Ah, *ma chère*! I really must tell you, I don't get any pleasure out of those large half-gnawed bones our Polkan likes guzzling in the kitchen. I only like bones from game-birds, and then only if the marrow hasn't already been sucked out by someone else. A mixture of several different sauces can be very tasty, as long as you don't put any capers or greens in. But in my opinion there's nothing worse than little pellets of dough. There's usually some gentleman sitting at the table who starts kneading bread with hands that not long before have been in contact with all sorts of filth. He'll call you over and stick a pellet between your teeth. It's rather bad manners to refuse, and you have to eat it though it's quite disgusting . . .'

What on earth does all that mean? Never read such rubbish! As if they didn't have anything better to write about! Let's look at another page and see if we can find something with a bit more sense in it.

'I should be delighted to tell you about everything that goes on in our house. I've already mentioned something about the head of the house, whom Sophie calls Papa. He's a very strange man.'

Ah, at last! Yes, I knew it all the time: their approach is very diplomatic. Let's see what they say about this Papa.

'. . . a very strange man. Says nothing most of the time. He speaks very rarely; but a week ago he kept on saying to himself: "Will I get it, will I get it?" Once he turned to me and asked, "What do you think, Medji? Will I get it, or won't I?" I couldn't understand a word he was saying. I sniffed his shoes and left the room. Then, *ma chère*, about a week later he came home beaming all over. The whole morning men in uniforms kept arriving to congratulate him on something or other. During dinner Papa was gayer than ever I'd seen him before, telling anecdotes, and afterwards lifting me up to his shoulders and saying: "Look, Medji, what's that?" It was some sort of ribbon. I sniffed at it, but it didn't have any sort of smell at all. Then I gave it a furtive lick, and it tasted rather salty.'

Hm! That dog, in my opinion, is going too far . . . She'll be lucky if she doesn't get a whipping! Ah, he's so ambitious! Must make a note of that.

'Goodbye, *ma chère*. I'm in a tearing hurry, etc. etc. . . . I'll finish the letter tomorrow. Well, hello, here I am again. Today my mistress Sophie . . .'

Aha! Let's see what she says about Sophie. Ah, you devil! Never mind, never mind . . . Let's get on with it.

'. . . my mistress Sophie was in such a tizzy. She was getting dressed for a ball, and I was delighted to have the chance of writing to you while she was gone. My Sophie is always thrilled to go to a ball, although getting ready usually puts her in a bad temper. I really can't understand, *ma chère*, what pleasure there is in going to these balls. Sophie comes home about six in the morning, and I can always tell from the poor dear's pale, thin look that she's had nothing to eat. I must confess *that* would be no life for me. If I didn't have woodcock

28

done in sauce or roast chicken wings I don't know what would become of me . . . Sauce goes very well with gruel. But you can't do anything with carrots or turnips, or artichokes . . .'

The style is amazingly jerky. You can see at once that it's not written by a human being. It starts off all right, and then lapses into dogginess . . . Let's have a look at another letter. Seems rather long. Hm, there's no date either!

'Ah, my dear, how deeply I feel the approach of spring! My heart is beating as though it were waiting for something. There's a perpetual noise in my ears, and I often raise a paw and stand listening at the door for several minutes. In confidence, I must tell you I have a great many suitors. I often sit watching them out of the window. Ah, if you only knew how ugly some of them are! There's one very coarse mongrel, so stupid you can see it written all over his face, and he swaggers down the street thinking he's someone very important and that everyone else thinks the same. But he's wrong. I ignored him completely, just as if I'd never set eyes on him. And that terrifying Great Dane that keeps stopping by my window! If he stood on his hind legs (the coarse clodhopper's not even capable of that) he'd be a whole head taller than Sophie's Papa – and as you know, *he's* tall enough – and plump into the bargain. The great lump has the cheek of the devil. I growled at him, but a fat lot he cared. He just frowned back, stuck his tongue out, dangled his enormous ears and kept staring straight at the window – the peasant! But don't imagine, *ma chère*, that my heart is indifferent to all these suitors, ah, no . . . If you'd seen one gallant called Trésor, who climbed over the fence from next door. Ah my dear, you should see his little muzzle!'

Ugh, to hell with it! What trash! Fancy filling a letter with such nonsense! I need *people*, not dogs! I want to see a human being; I ask for spiritual nourishment to feed and delight my soul, but all I end up with is that rubbish! Let's skip a page and see if there's something better.

'Sophie was sitting at a small table and sewing. I was looking out of the window as I love to see who's going by. All of a sudden a footman came into the room and said: "Teplov." "Ask him in," cried Sophie and threw her arms around me. "Ah, Medji, Medji, if you could only see him: a Guards Officer with brown hair, and his eyes – what eyes! – black, and shining bright as fire!"

'Sophie ran up to her room. A minute later in came a young gentleman with black whiskers. He went up to the mirror, smoothed his hair and looked round the room. I snarled and settled down by the window. Soon Sophie appeared and gaily curtseyed as he clicked his heels. I kept looking out of the window just as if they weren't there, but I tried to catch what they were saying by cocking my head to one side. Ah, *ma chère*! What rubbish they talked! About a certain lady who danced the wrong step at a ball, and someone called Bobov who looked just like a stork in his jabot, and who nearly fell over. And there was someone called Lidina who thought she had blue eyes, whereas they were really green, and so on. How can one compare, I asked myself, this gentleman of the court with Trésor? Good heavens, they're whole worlds apart! First of all, the young gentleman's face is wide and very smooth and has whiskers growing all round it, just as if someone had bound it up with a black handkerchief. But Trésor's muzzle is very thin, and he has a white spot on his forehead. And you can't compare their figures. And Trésor's eyes, his bearing, aren't the same at all. What a difference! I really don't what she can see in this court chamberlain. Why is she so crazy about him?

It strikes me something's not quite right here. How can a young court chamberlain sweep her off her feet like that? Let's have a look:

'I think that if she can care for that court chamberlain then she can easily feel the same for the civil servant who has a desk in Papa's study. Ah, *ma chère*, if only you knew how ugly he is! Just like a tortoise in a sack.'

What is this civil servant like?

'He has a very peculiar name. All the time he sits sharpening quills. His hair looks just like hay. Papa always sends him on errands instead of one of the servants.'

I think that nasty little dog is referring to me. Who says my hair is like hay?

'Sophie can't stop laughing when she looks at him.'

You damned dog, you're lying! You've got a wicked tongue! As if I didn't know you're jealous! And who's responsible for this? Why, the head of the department! That man has vowed undying hatred for me and does me harm whenever he has the chance. Let's see though: there's one more letter. Perhaps the explanation's there:

'*Ma chère* Fidèle, please forgive me for being so long writing to you. I have been in raptures. The author who said love is a second life was absolutely right. Great changes have been taking place in our house. The gentleman of the court comes every day now. Sophie is madly in love with him. Papa is in very high spirits. I even heard from Grigory (one of our servants who sweeps the floor and seems to be talking to himself all the time) that the wedding's going to be very soon. Papa is set on marrying off Sophie either to a general, or a court chamberlain, or a colonel . . .'

Damnation! I can't read any more . . . It's always noblemen or generals. All the good things in this world go to gentlemen of the court or generals. People like me scrape up a few crumbs of happiness and just as you're about to reach out to grasp them, along comes a nobleman or a general to snatch them away. Hell! I'd like to be a general, not just to win her, and all the rest of it, but to see them crawling around after me, with all their puns and high and mighty jokes from the court. Then I could tell them all to go to hell. Damn it! It's enough to make you weep. I tore that stupid little dog's letter into little bits.

December 3rd

It's impossible! What twaddle! There just *can't* be a wedding.
And what if he *is* a gentleman of the court? It's only a kind of
distinction conferred on you, not something that you can see,
or touch with your hands. A court chamberlain doesn't have a
third eye in the middle of his forehead, and his nose isn't made
of gold either. It's just like mine or anyone else's: he uses it to
sniff or sneeze with, but not for coughing. Several times I've
tried to discover the reason for these differences. Why am I
just a titular councillor?* Perhaps I'm really a count or a general
and am merely imagining I'm a titular councillor? Perhaps I
don't really know who I am at all? History has lots of examples
of that sort of thing: there was some fairly ordinary man, not
what you'd call a nobleman, but simply a tradesman or even
a serf, and suddenly he discovered he was a great lord or a
baron. So if a peasant can turn into someone like that, what
would a nobleman become? Say, for example, I suddenly
appeared in a general's uniform, with an epaulette on my left
shoulder and a blue sash across my chest – what then? What
tune would my beautiful young lady sing then? And Papa,
our Director? Oh, he's so ambitious! He must be a mason, no
doubt about that, although he pretends to be this, that and the
other; he only puts out two fingers to shake hands with. But
surely, can't I be promoted to Governor General or Commissary
or something or other this very minute? And I should like to
know why I'm a titular councillor? Why precisely a *titular*
councillor?

December 5th

I spent the whole morning reading the papers. Strange things
are happening in Spain. I read that the throne has been left
vacant and that the nobility are having a great deal of trouble

*Ninth grade in the bureaucratic structure. There were fourteen
grades altogether. (Trans.)

choosing an heir, with the result that there's a lot of civil commotion.* This strikes me as very strange. They're saying some 'donna' must succeed to the throne. But she can't succeed to the throne: that's impossible. A king must inherit the throne. And they say there's no king anyway. But there *must* be a king. There can't be a government without one. There's a king all right, but he's hiding in some obscure place. He must be somewhere, but is forced to stay in hiding for family reasons, or perhaps because he's in danger from some foreign country, such as France. Or there may be another explanation.

December 8th

I was about to go to the office but various reasons and considerations held me back. I couldn't get that Spanish business out of my head. How could a woman inherit the throne? They wouldn't allow it. Firstly, England wouldn't stand for it. And what's more, it would affect the whole of European policy: the Austrian Emperor, our Tsar, . . . I must confess, these events shook me up so much I couldn't put my mind to anything all day. Mavra pointed out that I was very absent-minded during supper. And, in fact, in a fit of distraction I threw two plates on to the floor, and they broke immediately. After dinner I walked along a street that led downhill. Discovered nothing very edifying. Afterwards I lay on my bed for a long time and pondered the Spanish question.

April 43rd, 2000

Today is a day of great triumph. There *is* a king of Spain. He has been found at last. That king is *me*. I only discovered this today. Frankly, it all came to me in a flash. I cannot understand

* Gogol is referring to the dispute over the succession to Ferdinand VII who died in 1833. (Trans.)

how I could even think or imagine for one moment I was only a titular councillor. I can't explain how such a ridiculous idea ever entered my head. Anyway, I'm rather pleased no one's thought of having me put away yet. The path ahead is clear: everything is as bright as daylight.

I don't really understand why, but before this revelation everything was enveloped in a kind of mist. And the whole reason for this, as I see it, is that people are under the misapprehension that the human brain is situated in the head: nothing could be further from the truth. It is carried by the wind from the Caspian Sea.

The first thing I did was to tell Mavra who I was. When she heard that the King of Spain was standing before her, she wrung her hands and nearly died of fright. The stupid woman had obviously *never* set eyes on the King of Spain before. However, I managed to calm her and with a few kind words tried to convince her that the new sovereign was well-disposed towards her and that I wasn't at all annoyed because she sometimes made a mess of my shoes.

But what can you expect from the common herd? You just can't converse with them about the higher things in life. Mavra was frightened because she was sure all kings of Spain looked like Philip II. But I explained that there was no resemblance between me and Philip and that I didn't have a single Capuchin friar under my sway . . . Didn't go to the office today. To hell with them! No, my friends, you won't tempt me now. I've had enough of copying out your filthy documents!

86th Martober, between day and night

One of the administrative clerks called today, saying it was time I went to the office and that I hadn't been for three weeks. So I went – just for a joke. The head clerk thought I would bow to him and start apologizing, but I gave him a cool look, not too hostile, but not too friendly either. I sat down at my desk as though no one else existed. As I looked at all that clerical scum I thought: 'If only you knew who's sitting in the same office with you . . . God, what a fuss you'd make! Even the head clerk himself would start bowing and scraping, just as he does when the Director's there.' They put some papers in front of me, from which I was supposed to make an abstract. But I didn't so much as lift a finger. A few minutes later everyone was rushing around like mad. They said the Director was coming. Many of the clerks jostled each other as they tried to be first to bow to him as he came in. But I didn't budge. Everyone buttoned up his jacket as the Director walked across the office, but I didn't make a move. So he's a departmental director, what of it? He's really a *cork*, not a director. And an ordinary cork at that – a common or garden cork, and nothing else, the kind used for stopping bottles. What tickled me more than anything else was when they shoved a paper in front of me to sign. Of course, they were thinking I would sign myself as: Clerk No. So-and-so, right at the very bottom of the page. Well, let them think again! In the most important place, just where the Director puts his signature, I wrote 'Ferdinand VIII'. The awed silence that descended on everyone was amazing; but I merely waved my hand and said: 'There's really no need for this show of loyalty,' and I walked out.

I went straight to the Director's flat. He wasn't at home. The footman wouldn't let me in at first, but what I said to him made his arms drop limply to his side. I made my way straight to *her* boudoir. She was sitting in front of the mirror and she jumped up and stepped backwards. I didn't tell her, however, that I was the King of Spain. All I said was that happiness such as she had never imagined awaited her, and that we would be together, in spite of hostile plots against us. Then I thought I'd said enough and left. But how crafty women can be! Only then did it dawn on me what they are really like. So far, no one has ever discovered whom women are in love with. I was the first to solve this mystery: they are in love with the Devil.

And I'm not joking. While physicians write a lot of nonsense, saying they are this and that, the truth is, women are in love with the Devil, and no one else. Can you see that woman raising her lorgnette in the first tier of a theatre box? Do you think she's looking at that fat man with a medal? On the contrary, she's looking at the Devil standing behind his back. Now he's hiding in the medal and is beckoning her with his finger! She'll marry him, that's for certain. And all those clerks who curry favour everywhere they go, insisting they are patriots, when all they want is money from rents! They'd sell their own mother, or father, or God for money, the crawlers, the Judases! And all this ambition is caused by a little bubble under the tongue which contains a tiny worm about the size of a pinhead, and it's all the work of some barber living in Gorokhovaya Street. I can't remember his name for the moment but one thing I'm sure of is that with the help of an old mid-wife he wants to spread Mahommedanism throughout the world. And I've already heard tell that most of the people in France are now practising the faith.

No date. The day didn't have one

I walked incognito down Nevsky Avenue. His Imperial Majesty drove past. Every single person doffed his hat, and I followed suit. However, I didn't let out that I was the King of Spain. I considered it improper to reveal my true identity right there in the middle of the crowd, because, according to etiquette, I ought first to be presented at court. So far, the only thing that had stopped me was not having any royal clothes. If only I could get hold of a cloak. I would have gone to a tailor, but they're such asses. What's more they tend to neglect their work, preferring to take part in shady transactions, and most of them end up mending the roads. I decided to have a mantle made out of my new uniform, which I'd worn only twice. I decided to make it myself, so that those crooks shouldn't ruin it, and shut myself in my room so that nobody would see. I had to cut it all up with a pair of scissors, because the style's completely different.

I don't remember the date. There wasn't any month either. Damned if I know what it was.

The cloak is ready now. Mavra screamed when I put it on. But I still can't make up my mind whether to present myself at court. So far no deputation's arrived from Spain and it would be contrary to etiquette to go on my own. It would detract from my dignity. Anyway I'm expecting them any minute now.

The first

I'm really astonished the deputation's so slow in coming. Whatever can have held them up? Could it be France? Yes, she's extremely hostile at the moment. I went to the post office to see if there was any news about the Spanish deputation. But the postmaster was extremely stupid and knew nothing about it. 'No,' he said, 'no Spanish deputation has arrived but if you care to send a letter, it will be dispatched in the normal manner.'

To hell with it! Letters are trash. Only chemists write letters.

Madrid, 30th Februarius

So I'm in Spain now, and it was all so quick I hardly knew what was happening. This morning the Spanish deputation arrived and I got into a carriage with them. We drove very fast, and this struck me as most peculiar. In fact we went at such a cracking pace we were at the Spanish frontier within half an hour. But then, there are railways all over Europe now, and ships can move extremely fast. A strange country, Spain: in the first room I entered there were a lot of people with shaven heads. However, I guessed that these must either be grandees or soldiers, as they're in the habit of shaving their heads over there. But the way one of the government chancellors treated me was strange in the extreme. He took me by the arm and pushed me into a small room, saying: 'Sit there, and if you call yourself King Ferdinand once more, I'll thrash that nonsense out of you.' But as I knew that this was just some sort of test I refused, for which the chancellor struck me twice on the back, so painfully that I nearly cried out. But I controlled myself, as I knew that this was the normal procedure with Spanish knights before initiating someone into a very high rank and that even now the code of chivalry is still maintained over there. Left on my own I decided to get down to government business. I have discovered that China and Spain are really one and the same country, and it's only ignorance that leads people to think that they're two different nations. If you don't believe me, then try and write 'Spain' and you'll end up writing 'China'. Apart from all this, I'm very annoyed by an event that's due to take place at 7 o'clock tomorrow. A strange phenomenon: the earth is going to land on the moon. An account of this has been written by the celebrated English chemist Wellington.

I confess I felt deeply troubled when I considered how unusually delicate and insubstantial the moon is. The moon, as everyone knows, is usually made in Hamburg, and they make a complete hash of it. I'm surprised that the English don't do something about it. The moon is manufactured by a lame cooper, and it's obvious the idiot has no idea what it should be made of. The materials he uses are tarred rope and linseed oil. That's why there's such a terrible stink all over the earth, which makes us stop our noses up. And it also explains why the moon is such a delicate sphere, and why people can't live there – only noses. For this reason we can't see our own noses any more, as they're all on the moon. When I reflected how heavy the earth is and that our noses might be ground into the surface when it landed, I was so worried I put my socks and shoes on and hurried into the state council room to instruct the police not to let the earth land on the moon. The grandees with their shaven heads – the council chamber was chock-full of them – were a very clever lot, and as soon as I told them: 'Gentlemen, let us save the moon because the earth intends landing there,' everyone fell over himself to carry out my royal wish. Many of them went wild to reach the moon. But just at this moment in came the mighty chancellor. Everyone fled when they saw him. Being the king, I stayed where I was. But to my astonishment the chancellor hit me with his stick and drove me back into my room. That shows you how strong tradition is in Spain!

January in the same year falling after February

Up to this time Spain had been somewhat of a mystery to me. Their native customs and court etiquette are really most peculiar. I don't understand, I really do *not* understand them. Today they shaved my head even though I shrieked as loud as I could that I didn't want to be a monk. And I have only a faint memory of what happened when they poured cold water over my head. Never before had I gone through such hell. I was in such a frenzy they had difficulty in holding me down. What these strange customs mean is beyond me. So foolish, idiotic! And the utter stupidity of their kings who have still not abolished this tradition really defeats me. After everything that's happened to me, I think I'm safe in hazarding a guess that I've fallen into the hands of the Inquisition, and the person I thought was a minister of state was really the Grand Inquisitor himself. But I still don't understand how *kings* can be subjected to the Inquisition. It could of course be France that's putting them up to it, and I mean Polignac* in particular. What a

*Polignac was foreign minister under Charles X of France. He was chiefly responsible for the occupation of Algeria by the French during the 1830s. (Trans.)

swine he is! He's sworn to have me done away with. The whole time he's persecuting me; but I know very well, my friend, that you're led by the English. The English are acute politicians and worm their way into everything. The whole world knows that when England takes snuff, France sneezes.

The 25th

Today the Grand Inquisitor came into the room, but as soon as I heard his footsteps I hid under the table. When he saw I wasn't there, he started calling out. First he shouted: 'Poprishchin!' – I didn't say a word. Then: 'Axenty Ivanov! Titular Councillor! Nobleman!' – still I didn't reply. 'Ferdinand the Eighth, King of Spain!' I was in half a mind to stick my head out, but thought better of it. 'No, my friend, you can't fool me! I know only too well you're going to pour cold water over my head.' He spotted me all the same and drove me out from under the table with his stick. The damned thing is terribly painful. But my next discovery that every cock has its Spain, tucked away under its feathers, made up for all these torments. The Grand Inquisitor left in a very bad mood however and threatened me with some sort of punishment. But I didn't care a rap about his helpless rage, as I knew full well he was functioning like a machine, a mere tool of the English.

Da 34 te Mth eary ꭓɘᗡυɒɿʇ 349

No, I haven't the strength to endure it any longer! Good God, what are they doing to me? They're pouring cold water over my head! They won't listen to me or come and see me. What have I done to them? Why do they torture me so? What can they want from a miserable wretch like me? What can I offer them when I've nothing of my own? I can't stand this torture any more. My head is burning and everything is spinning round and round. Save me! Take me away! Give me a troika with horses swift as the whirlwind! Climb up, driver, and let the bells ring! Soar away, horses, and carry me from this world! Further, further, where nothing can be seen, nothing at all! Over there the sky whirls round. A little star shines in the distance; the forest rushes past with its dark trees and the moon shines above. A deep blue haze is spreading like a carpet; a guitar string twangs in the mist. On one side is the sea, on the other is Italy. And over there I can see Russian peasant huts. Is that my house looking dimly blue in the distance? And is that my mother sitting at the window? Mother, save your poor son! Shed a tear on his aching head! See how they're torturing him! Press a wretched orphan to your breast! There's no place for him in this world! They're persecuting him! Mother, have pity on your poor little child . . .

And did you know that the Dhey of Algiers* has a wart right under his nose?

*The reference is to Hussein Pasha, deposed by the French in 1830. (Trans.)

The Nose

AN extraordinarily strange thing happened in St Petersburg on 25 March. Ivan Yakovlevich, a barber who lived on Voznesensky Avenue (his surname has got lost and all that his shop-front signboard shows is a gentleman with a lathered cheek and the inscription 'We also let blood'), woke up rather early one morning and smelt hot bread. As he sat up in bed he saw his wife, who was a quite respectable lady and a great coffee-drinker, taking some freshly baked rolls out of the oven.

'I don't want any coffee today, Praskovya Osipovna,' said Ivan Yakovlevich, 'I'll make do with some hot rolls and onion instead.' (Here I must explain that Ivan Yakovlevich would really have liked to have had some coffee as well, but knew it was quite out of the question to expect both coffee *and* rolls, since Praskovya Osipovna did not take very kindly to these whims of his.) 'Let the old fool have his bread, I don't mind,' she thought. 'That means extra coffee for me!' And she threw a roll on to the table.

Ivan pulled his frock-coat over his nightshirt for decency's sake, sat down at the table, poured out some salt, peeled two onions, took a knife and with a determined expression on his face started cutting one of the rolls.

When he had sliced the roll in two, he peered into the middle and was amazed to see something white there. Ivan carefully picked at it with his knife, and felt it with his finger. 'Quite thick,' he said to himself. 'What on earth can it be?'

He poked two fingers in and pulled out – a nose!

He flopped back in his chair, and began rubbing his eyes and feeling around in the roll again. Yes, it was a nose all right, no mistake about that. And, what's more, it seemed a very familiar nose. His face filled with horror. But this horror was nothing compared with his wife's indignation.

'You beast, whose nose is *that* you've cut off?' she cried furiously. 'You scoundrel! You drunkard! I'll report it to the police myself, I will. You thief! Come to think of it, I've heard three customers say that when they come in for a shave you start pulling their noses about so much it's a wonder they stay on at all!'

But Ivan felt more dead than alive. He knew that the nose belonged to none other than Collegiate Assessor Kovalyov, whom he shaved on Wednesdays and Sundays.

'Wait a minute, Praskovya! I'll wrap it up in a piece of cloth and dump it in the corner. Let's leave it there for a bit, then I'll try and get rid of it.'

'I don't want to know! Do you think I'm going to let a sawn-off nose lie around in *my* room . . . you fathead! All you can do is strop that blasted razor of yours and let everything else go to pot. Layabout! Night-bird! And you expect me to cover up for you with the police! You filthy pig! Blockhead! Get that nose out of here, out! Do what you like with it, but I don't want that thing hanging around here a minute longer!'

Ivan Yakovlevich was absolutely stunned. He thought and thought, but just didn't know what to make of it.

'I'm damned if I know what's happened!' he said at last, scratching the back of his ear. 'I can't say for certain if I came home drunk or not last night. All I know is, it's crazy. After all, bread is baked in an oven, and you don't get noses in bakeries. Can't make head or tail of it! . . .'

Ivan Yakovlevich lapsed into silence. The thought that the police might search the place, find the nose and afterwards bring a charge against him, very nearly sent him out of his mind. Already he could see that scarlet collar beautifully embroidered with silver, that sword . . . and he began shaking all over. Finally he put on his scruffy old trousers and shoes and with Praskovya Osipovna's vigorous invective ringing in his ears, wrapped the nose up in a piece of cloth and went out into the street.

All he wanted was to stuff it away somewhere, either hiding it between two curb-stones by someone's front door or else 'accidentally' dropping it and slinking off down a side street. But as luck would have it, he kept bumping into friends, who would insist on asking: 'Where are *you* off to?' or 'It's a bit early for shaving customers, isn't it?' with the result that he didn't have a chance to get rid of it. Once he *did* manage to drop it, but a policeman pointed with his halberd and said: 'Pick that up! Can't you see you dropped something!' And Ivan Yakovlevich had to pick it up and hide it in his pocket. Despair gripped him, especially as the streets were getting more and more crowded now as the shops and stalls began to open.

He decided to make his way to St Isaac's Bridge and see if he could throw the nose into the River Neva without anyone seeing him. But here I am rather at fault for not telling you before something about Ivan Yakovlevich, who in many ways was a man you could respect.

Ivan Yakovlevich, like any honest Russian working man, was a terrible drunkard. And although he spent all day shaving other people's beards, he never touched his own. His frock-coat (Ivan Yakovlevich never wore a dress – coat) could best be described as piebald: that is to say, it was black, but with brownish-yellow and grey spots all over it. His collar was very shiny, and three loosely hanging threads showed that some buttons had once been there. Ivan Yakovlevich was a very phlegmatic character, and whenever Kovalyov the Collegiate Assessor said 'Your hands always stink!' while he was being shaved, Ivan Yakovlevich would say: 'But why *should* they stink?' The Collegiate Assessor used to reply: 'Don't ask me, my dear chap. All I know is, they *stink*.' Ivan Yakovlevich would answer by taking a pinch of snuff and then, by way of retaliation, lather all over Kovalyov's cheeks, under his nose, behind the ears and beneath his beard – in short, wherever he felt like covering him with soap.

By now this respectable citizen of ours had already reached St Isaac's Bridge. First of all he had a good look round. Then he leant over the rails, trying to pretend he was looking under the bridge to see if there were many fish there, and furtively threw the packet into the water. He felt as if a couple of hundredweight had been lifted from his shoulders and he even managed to produce a smile.

Instead of going off to shave civil servants' chins, he headed for a shop bearing the sign 'Hot Meals and Tea' for a glass of punch. Suddenly he saw a policeman at one end of the bridge, in a very smart uniform, with broad whiskers, a three-cornered hat and a sword. He went cold all over as the policeman beckoned to him and said: 'Come here, my friend!'

Recognizing the uniform, Ivan Yakovlevich took his cap off before he had taken half a dozen steps, tripped up to him and greeted him with: 'Good morning, Your Excellency!'

'No, no, my dear chap, none of your "Excellencies". Just tell me what you were up to on the bridge?'

'Honest, officer, I was on my way to shave a customer and stopped to see how fast the current was.'

'You're lying. You really can't expect me to believe that! You'd better come clean at once!'

'I'll give Your Excellency a free shave twice, even three times a week, honest I will,' answered Ivan Yakovlevich.

'No, no, my friend, that won't do. Three barbers look after me already, and it's an *honour* for them to shave me. Will you please tell me what you were up to?'

Ivan Yakovlevich turned pale ... But at this point everything became so completely enveloped in mist it is really impossible to say what happened afterwards.

Collegiate Assessor Kovalyov woke up rather early and made a 'brring' noise with his lips. He always did this when he woke up, though, if you asked him why, he could not give any good reason. Kovalyov stretched himself and asked for the small mirror that stood on the table to be brought over to him. He wanted to have a look at a pimple that had made its appearance on his nose the previous evening, but to his extreme astonishment found that instead of a nose there was nothing but an absolutely flat surface! In a terrible panic Kovalyov asked for some water and rubbed his eyes with a towel. No mistake about it: his nose had gone. He began pinching himself to make sure he was not sleeping, but to all intents and purposes he was wide awake. Collegiate Assessor Kovalyov sprang out of bed and shook himself: still no nose! He asked for his clothes and off he dashed straight to the Head of Police.

In the meantime, however, a few words should be said about Kovalyov, so that the reader may see what kind of collegiate assessor this man was. You really cannot compare those collegiate assessors who acquire office through testimonials with the variety appointed in the Caucasus. The two species are quite distinct. Collegiate assessors with diplomas from learned bodies . . . But Russia is such an amazing country, that if you pass any remark about *one* collegiate assessor, every assessor from Riga to Kamchatka will take it personally. And the same goes for all people holding titles and government ranks. Kovalyov belonged to the Caucasian variety.

He had been a collegiate assessor for only two years and therefore could not forget it for a single minute. To make himself sound more important and to give more weight to his status he never called himself collegiate assessor, but 'Major'. If he met a woman in the street selling shirt fronts he would say: 'Listen dear, come and see me at home. My flat's in

Sadovaya Street. All you have to do is ask if Major Kovalyov lives there and anyone will show you the way.' And if the woman was at all pretty he would whisper some secret instructions and then say: 'Just ask for Major Kovalyov, my dear.' Therefore, throughout this story, we will call this collegiate assessor 'Major'. Major Kovalyov was in the habit of taking a daily stroll along the Nevsky Avenue. His shirt collar was always immaculately clean and well-starched. His whiskers were the kind you usually find among provincial surveyors, architects and regimental surgeons, among people who have some sort of connection with the police, on anyone in fact who has full rosy cheeks and plays a good hand at whist. These whiskers grew right from the middle of his cheeks up to his nostrils. Major Kovalyov always carried plenty of seals with him – seals bearing coats of arms or engraved with the words: 'Wednesday, Thursday, Monday,' and so on. Major Kovalyov had come to St Petersburg with the set purpose of finding a position in keeping with his rank. If he was lucky, he would get a vice-governorship, but failing that, a job as an administrative clerk in some important government department would have to do. Major Kovalyov was not averse to marriage, as long as his bride happened to be worth 200,000 roubles. And now the reader can judge for himself how this Major felt when, instead of a fairly presentable and reasonably sized nose, all he saw was an absolutely preposterous smooth flat space.

As if this were not bad enough, there was not a cab in sight, and he had to walk home, keeping himself huddled up in his cloak and with a handkerchief over his face to make people think he was bleeding. 'But perhaps I dreamt it! How could I be so stupid as to go and lose my nose?' With these thoughts he dropped into a coffee-house to take a look at himself in a mirror. Fortunately the shop was empty, except for some waiters sweeping up and tidying the chairs. A few of them, rather bleary-eyed, were carrying trays laden with hot pies. Yesterday's newspapers, covered in coffee stains, lay scattered on the tables and chairs. 'Well, thank God there's no one about,' he said. 'Now I can have a look.' He approached the mirror rather gingerly and peered into it. 'Damn it! What kind of trick is this?' he cried, spitting on the floor. 'If only there were *something* to take its place, but there's nothing!'

He bit his lips in annoyance, left the coffee-house and decided not to smile or look at anyone, which was not like him at all. Suddenly he stood rooted to the spot near the front door of some house and witnessed a most incredible sight. A carriage drew up at the entrance porch. The doors flew open and out jumped a uniformed, stooping gentleman who dashed up the steps. The feeling of horror and amazement that gripped Kovalyov when he recognized his own nose defies description! After this extraordinary sight everything went topsy-turvy. He could hardly keep to his feet, but decided at all costs to wait until the nose returned to the carriage, although he was shaking all over and felt quite feverish.

About two minutes later a nose really did come out. It was wearing a gold-braided uniform with a high stand-up collar and chamois trousers, and had a sword at its side. From the plumes on its hat one could tell that it held the exalted rank of state councillor.* And it was abundantly clear that the nose was going to visit someone. It looked right, then left, shouted to the coachman 'Let's go!', climbed in and drove off.

Poor Kovalyov nearly went out of his mind. He did not know what to make of it. How, in fact, could a nose, which only yesterday was in the middle of his face, and which could not possibly walk around or drive in a carriage, suddenly turn up in a uniform! He ran after the carriage which fortunately did not travel very far and came to a halt outside Kazan Cathedral.† Kovalyov rushed into the cathedral square,

*A state councillor held the fifth of the fourteen ranks in the civil service hierarchy. A collegiate assessor was three grades lower. (Trans.)

† Such was the severity and idiocy of the censorship in Gogol's day, that in the original version Kazan Cathedral had to be replaced by a shopping arcade, on the grounds of 'blasphemy'. (Trans.)

48

elbowed his way through a crowd of beggar women who always used to make him laugh because of the way they covered their faces, leaving only slits for the eyes, and made his way in. Only a few people were at prayer, all of them standing by the entrance. Kovalyov felt so distraught that he was in no condition for praying, and his eyes searched every nook and cranny for the nose in uniform. At length he spotted it standing by one of the walls to the side. The nose's face was completely hidden by the high collar and it was praying with an expression of profound piety.

'What's the best way of approaching it?' thought Kovalyov. 'Judging by its uniform, its hat, and its whole appearance, it must be a state councillor. But I'm damned if I know!'

He tried to attract its attention by coughing, but the nose did not interrupt its devotions for one second and continued bowing towards the altar.

'My dear sir,' Kovalyov said, summoning up his courage, 'my dear sir . . .'

'What do you want?' replied the nose, turning round.

'I don't know how best to put it, sir, but it strikes me as very peculiar . . . Don't you know where you belong? And where do I find you? In church, of all places! I'm sure you'll agree that . . .'

'Please forgive me, but would you mind telling me what you're talking about? . . . Explain yourself.'

'How can I make myself clear?' Kovalyov wondered. Nerving himself once more he said: 'Of course, I am, as it happens, a Major. You will agree that it's not done for someone in my position to walk around minus a nose. It's all right for some old woman selling peeled oranges on the Voskresensky Bridge to go around without one. But as I'm hoping to be promoted soon . . . Besides, as I'm acquainted with several highly-placed ladies: Madame Chekhtaryev, for example, a state councillor's wife . . . you can judge for yourself . . . I really don't know what to say, my dear sir . . . (He shrugged his shoulders as he said this.) Forgive me, but you must look upon this as a matter of honour and principle. You can see for yourself . . .'

'I can't see anything,' the nose replied. 'Please come to the point.'

'My dear sir,' continued Kovalyov in a smug voice, 'I really don't know what you mean by that. It's plain enough for anyone to see . . . Unless you want . . . Don't you realize you are *my own nose*!'

The nose looked at the Major and frowned a little.

'My dear fellow, you are mistaken. I am a person in my own right. Furthermore, I don't see that we can have anything in common. Judging from your uniform buttons, I should say you're from another government department.'

With these words the nose turned away and continued its prayers.

Kovalyov was so confused he did not know what to do or think. At that moment he heard the pleasant rustling of a woman's dress, and an elderly lady, bedecked with lace, came by, accompanied by a slim girl wearing a white dress, which showed her shapely figure to very good advantage, and a pale yellow hat as light as pastry. A tall footman, with enormous whiskers and what seemed to be a dozen collars, stationed himself behind them and opened his snuff-box. Kovalyov went closer, pulled the linen collar of his shirt front up high, straightened the seals hanging on his gold watch chain and, smiling all over his face, turned his attention to the slim girl, who bent over to pray like a spring flower and kept lifting her little white hand with its almost transparent fingers to her forehead.

The smile on Kovalyov's face grew even more expansive when he saw, beneath her hat, a little rounded chin of dazzling white, and cheeks flushed with the colour of the first rose of spring.

But suddenly he jumped backwards as though he had been

burnt: he remembered that instead of a nose he had nothing, and tears streamed from his eyes. He turned round to tell the nose in uniform straight out that it was only masquerading as a state councillor, that it was an impostor and a scoundrel, and really nothing else than his own private property, *his* nose . . . But the nose had already gone: it had managed to slip off unseen, probably to pay somebody a visit.

This reduced Kovalyov to absolute despair. He went out, and stood for a minute or so under the colonnade, carefully looking around him in the hope of spotting the nose. He remembered quite distinctly that it was wearing a plumed hat and a gold-embroidered uniform. But he had not noticed what its greatcoat was like, or the colour of its carriage, or its horses, or even if there was a liveried footman at the back. What's more, there were so many carriages careering to and fro, so fast, that it was practically impossible to recognize any of them, and even if he could, there was no way of making them stop.

It was a beautiful sunny day. Nevsky Avenue was packed. From the Police Headquarters right down to the Anichkov Bridge people flowed along the pavements in a cascade of colour. Not far off he could see that court councillor whom he referred to as Lieutenant-Colonel,* especially if there happened to be other people around. And over there was Yaygin, a head clerk in the Senate, and a very close friend of his who always lost at whist when he played in a party of eight. Another Major, a collegiate assessor, of the Caucasian variety, waved to him to come over and have a chat.

'Blast and damn!' said Kovalyov, hailing a drozhky. 'Driver, take me straight to the Chief of Police.'

He climbed into the drozhky and shouted: 'Drive like the devil!'

'Is the Police Commissioner in?' he said as soon as he entered the hall.

*The civil service ranks had their corresponding ranks in the army. (Trans.)

'No, he's not, sir,' said the porter. 'He left only a few minutes ago.'

'This really *is* my day.'

'Yes,' added the porter, 'you've only just missed him. A minute ago you'd have caught him.'

Kovalyov, his handkerchief still pressed to his face, climbed into the drozhky again and cried out in a despairing voice: 'Let's go!'

'Where?' asked the driver.

'Straight on!'

'Straight on? But it's a dead-end here – you can only go right or left.'

This last question made Kovalyov stop and think. In his position the best thing to do was to go first to the City Security Office, not because it was directly connected with the police, but because things got done there much quicker than in any other government department. There was no sense in going direct to the head of the department where the nose claimed to work since anyone could see from the answers he had got before that the nose considered nothing holy and would have no difficulty in convincing its superiors by its brazen lying that it had never set eyes on Kovalyov before.

So just as Kovalyov was about to tell the driver to go straight to the Security Office, it struck him that the scoundrel and impostor who had behaved so shamelessly could quite easily take advantage of the delay and slip out of the city, in which event all his efforts to find it would be futile and might even drag on for another month, God forbid. Finally inspiration came from above. He decided to go straight to the newspaper offices and publish an advertisement, giving such a detailed description of the nose that anyone who happened to meet it would at once turn it over to Kovalyov, or at least tell him where he could find it. Deciding this was the best course of action, he ordered the driver to go straight to the newspaper offices and throughout the whole journey never once stopped pummelling the driver in the back with his fist and shouting: 'Faster, damn you, faster!'

'But sir ...' the driver retorted as he shook his head and flicked his reins at his horse, which had a coat as long as a spaniel's. Finally the drozhky came to a halt and the breathless Kovalyov tore into a small waiting-room where a grey-haired bespectacled clerk in an old frock-coat was sitting at a table with his pen between his teeth, counting out copper coins.

'Who sees to advertisements here?' Kovalyov shouted. 'Ah, good morning.'

'Good morning,' replied the grey-haired clerk, raising his eyes for one second, then looking down again at the little piles of money spread out on the table.

'I want to publish an advertisement.'

'Just one moment, if you don't mind,' the clerk answered, as he wrote down a figure with one hand and moved two beads on his abacus with the other.

A footman who, judging by his gold-braided livery and generally very smart appearance, obviously worked in some noble house, was standing by the table holding a piece of paper and, just to show he could hob-nob with high and low, started rattling away:

'Believe me, that nasty little dog just isn't worth eighty kopecks. I wouldn't give more than sixteen for it. But the Countess dotes on it, and that's why she makes no bones about offering a hundred roubles to the person who finds it. If we're going to be honest with one another, I'll tell you quite openly, there's no accounting for taste. I can understand a fancier paying anything up to five hundred, even a thousand for a deerhound or a poodle, as long as it's a good dog.'

The elderly clerk listened to him solemnly while he carried on totting up the words in the advertisement. The room was crowded with old women, shopkeepers, and house-porters, all holding advertisements. In one of these a coachman of 'sober disposition' was seeking employment; in another a carriage,

53

hardly used, and brought from Paris in 1814, was up for sale; in another a nineteen-year-old servant-girl, with laundry experience, and prepared to do *other* work, was looking for a job. Other advertisements offered a drozhky for sale – in good condition apart from one missing spring; a 'young' and spirited dapple-grey colt seventeen years old; radish and turnip seeds only just arrived from London; a country house, with every modern convenience, including stabling for two horses and enough land for planting an excellent birch or fir forest. And one invited prospective buyers of old boot soles to attend certain auction rooms between the hours of eight and three daily. The room into which all these people were crammed was small and extremely stuffy. But Collegiate Assessor Kovalyov could not smell anything as he had covered his face with a handkerchief – and he could not have smelt anything anyway, as his nose had disappeared God knows where.

'My dear sir, will you take the details down now, *please*. I really can't wait any longer,' he said, beginning to lose patience.

'Just a minute, if you *don't* mind! Two roubles forty-three kopecks. Nearly ready. One rouble sixty-four kopecks,' the grey-haired clerk muttered as he shoved pieces of paper at the old ladies and servants standing around. Finally he turned to Kovalyov and said: 'What do you want?'

'I want . . .' Kovalyov began. 'Something very fishy's been going on, whether it's some nasty practical joke or a plain case of fraud I can't say as yet. All I want you to do is to offer a substantial reward for the first person to find the blackguard . . .'

'Name, please.'

'Why do you need that? I can't tell you. Too many people know me – Mrs Chekhtaryev, for example, who's married to a state councillor, Mrs Palageya Podtochin, a staff officer's wife . . . they'd find out who it was at once, God forbid! Just put "Collegiate Assessor", or even better, "Major".'

'And the missing person was a household serf of yours?'

'Household serf? The crime wouldn't be half as serious! It's my *nose* that's disappeared.'

'Hm, strange name. And did this Mr Nose steal much?'

'*My* nose, I'm trying to say. You don't understand! It's my own nose that's disappeared. It's a diabolical practical joke someone's played on me.'

'How did it disappear? I don't follow.'

'I can't tell you how. But please understand, my nose is travelling at this very moment all over the town, calling itself a state councillor. That's why I'm asking you to print this advertisement announcing the first person who catches it should return the nose to its rightful owner as soon as possible. Imagine what it's like being without such a conspicuous part of your body! If it were just a small toe, then I could put my shoe on and no one would be any the wiser. On Thursdays I go to Mrs Chekhtaryev's (she's married to a state councillor) and Mrs Podtochin, who has a staff officer for a husband – and a very pretty little daughter as well. They're all very close friends of mine, so just imagine what it would be like . . . In *my* state how can I visit any of them?'

The clerk's tightly pressed lips showed he was deep in thought. 'I can't print an advertisement like that in our paper,' he said after a long silence.

'What? Why not?'

'I'll tell you. A paper can get a bad name. If everyone started announcing his nose had run away, I don't know how it would all end. And enough false reports and rumours get past editorial already . . .'

'But why does it strike you as so absurd? *I* certainly don't think so.'

'That's what *you* think. But only last week there was a similar case. A clerk came here with an advertisement, just like you. It cost him two roubles seventy-three kopecks, and all he wanted to advertise was a runaway black poodle. And what do you think he was up to really? In the end we had a libel case on our hands: the poodle was meant as a satire on a government cashier – I can't remember what ministry he came from.'

'But I want to publish an advertisement about my nose, not a poodle, and that's as near myself as dammit!'

'No, I can't accept that kind of advertisement.'

'But I've lost my *nose*!'

'Then you'd better see a doctor about it. I've heard there's a certain kind of specialist who can fix you up with any kind of nose you like. Anyway, you seem a cheery sort, and I can see you like to have your little joke.'

'By all that's holy, I swear I'm telling you the truth. If you really want me to, I'll *show* you what I mean.'

'I shouldn't bother if I were you,' the clerk continued, taking a pinch of snuff. 'However, if it's *really* no trouble,' he added, leaning forward out of curiosity, 'then I shouldn't mind having a quick look.'

The collegiate assessor removed his handkerchief.

'Well, how very peculiar! It's quite flat, just like a freshly cooked pancake. Incredibly flat.'

'So much for your objections! Now you've seen it with your own eyes and you can't possibly refuse. I will be particularly grateful for this little favour, and it's been a real pleasure meeting you.'

The Major, evidently, had decided that flattery might do the trick.

'Of course, it's no problem *printing* the advertisement,' the clerk said. 'But I can't see what you can stand to gain by it. If you like, why not give it to someone with a flair for journalism, then he can write it up as a very rare freak of nature and have it published in *The Northern Bee** (here he took another pinch of snuff) so that young people might benefit from it (here he wiped his nose). Or else, as something of interest to the general public.'

*A reactionary St Petersburg periodical notorious for its vicious attacks on writers of talent, including Gogol. (Trans.)

The collegiate assessor's hopes vanished completely. He looked down at the bottom of the page at the theatre guide. The name of a rather pretty actress almost brought a smile to his face, and he reached down to his pocket to see if he had a five-rouble note, since in his opinion staff officers should sit only in the stalls. But then he remembered his nose, and knew he could not possibly think of going to the theatre.

Apparently even the clerk was touched by Kovalyov's terrible predicament and thought it would not hurt to cheer him up with a few words of sympathy.

'Really, I can't say how sorry I am at what's happened. How about a pinch of snuff? It's very good for headaches – and puts fresh heart into you. It even cures piles.'

With these words he offered Kovalyov his snuff-box, deftly flipping back the lid which bore a portrait of some lady in a hat.

This unintentionally thoughtless action made Kovalyov lose patience altogether.

'I don't understand how you can joke at a time like this,' he said angrily. 'Are you so blind you can't see that I've nothing to smell with? You know what you can do with your snuff! I can't bear to look at it, and anyway you might at least offer me some real French rapée, not that filthy Berezinsky brand.'

After this declaration he strode furiously out of the newspaper office and went off to the local Inspector of Police (a fanatical lover of sugar, whose hall and dining room were crammed full of sugar-cubes presented by merchants who wanted to keep well in with him). Kovalyov arrived just when he was having a good stretch, grunting, and saying, 'Now for a nice two hours' nap.' Our collegiate assessor had clearly chosen a very bad time for his visit.

The Inspector was a great patron of the arts and industry, but most of all he loved government banknotes. 'There's nothing finer than banknotes,' he used to say. 'They don't need feeding, take up very little room and slip nicely into the pocket. And they don't break if you drop them.'

The Inspector gave Kovalyov a rather cold welcome and said that after dinner wasn't at all the time to start investigations, that nature herself had decreed a rest after meals (from this our collegiate assessor concluded the Inspector was well versed in the wisdom of antiquity), that *respectable* men do not get their noses ripped off, and that there were no end of majors knocking around who were not too fussy about their underwear and who were in the habit of visiting the most disreputable places.

These few home truths stung Kovalyov to the quick. Here I must point out that Kovalyov was an extremely sensitive man. He did not so much mind people making personal remarks about him, but it was a different matter when aspersions were cast on his rank or social standing.

As far as he was concerned they could say what they liked about subalterns on the stage, but staff officers should be exempt from attack.

The reception given him by the Inspector startled him so much that he shook his head, threw out his arms and said in a dignified voice, 'To be frank, after these remarks of yours, which I find very offensive, I have nothing more to say ...' and walked out. He arrived home hardly able to feel his feet beneath him. It was already getting dark. After his fruitless inquiries his flat seemed extremely dismal and depressing. As he entered the hall he saw his footman Ivan lying on a soiled leather couch spitting at the ceiling, managing to hit the same spot with a fair degree of success. The nonchalance of the man infuriated him and Kovalyov hit him across the forehead with his hat and said: 'You fat pig! Haven't you anything better to do!'

Ivan promptly jumped up and rushed to take off Kovalyov's coat. Tired and depressed, the Major went to his room, threw himself into an armchair and after a few sighs said:

'My God, my God! What have I done to deserve this? If I'd lost an arm or a leg it wouldn't be so bad. Even without any *ears* things wouldn't be very pleasant, but it wouldn't be the end of the world. A man without a nose, though, is God knows what, neither fish nor fowl. Just something to be thrown out of the window. If my nose had been lopped off during the war, or in a duel, at least I might have had some say in the matter. But to lose it for no reason at all and with nothing to show for it, not even a kopeck! No, it's absolutely impossible . . . It can't have gone just like that! Never! Must have been a dream, or perhaps I drank some of that vodka I use for rubbing down my beard after shaving instead of water: that idiot Ivan couldn't have put it back in the cupboard.'

To prove to himself he was not drunk the Major pinched himself so hard that he cried out in pain, which really did convince him he was awake and in full possession of his senses. He stealthily crept over to the mirror and screwed up his eyes in the hope that his nose would reappear in its proper place, but at once he jumped back, exclaiming:

'That ridiculous blank space again!'

It was absolutely incomprehensible. If a button, or a silver spoon, or his watch, or something of that sort had been missing, that would have been understandable. But for his *nose* to disappear from his own flat . . . Major Kovalyov weighed up all the evidence and decided that the most likely explanation of all was that Mrs Podtochin, the staff officer's wife, who wanted to marry off her daughter to him, was to blame, and no one else. In fact he liked chasing after her, but never came to proposing. And when the staff officer's wife used to tell him straight out that she was offering him her daughter's hand, he would politely withdraw, excusing himself on the grounds that he was still a young man, and that he wanted to devote another five years to the service, by which time he would be just forty-two. So, to get her revenge, the staff officer's wife must have hired some witches to spirit it away, and this was the only way his nose could possibly have been cut off – no one had visited him in his flat, his barber

59

Ivan Yakovlevich had shaved him only last Wednesday, and the rest of that day and the whole of Thursday his nose had been intact. All this he remembered quite clearly. Moreover, he would have been in pain and the wound could not have healed as smooth as a pancake in such a short time. He began planning what to do: either he would sue the staff officer's wife for damages, or he would go and see her personally and accuse her point blank.

But he was distracted from these thoughts by the sight of some chinks of light in the door, which meant Ivan had lit a candle in the hall. Soon afterwards Ivan appeared in person, holding the candle in front of him, so that it brightened up the whole room. Kovalyov's first reaction was to seize his handkerchief and cover up the bare place where only yesterday his nose had been, to prevent that stupid idiot from standing there gaping at him. No sooner had Ivan left than a strange voice was heard in the hall:

'Does Collegiate Assessor Kovalyov live here?'

'Please come in. The Major's home,' said Kovalyov, springing to his feet and opening the door.

A smart-looking police officer, with plump cheeks and whiskers that were neither too light nor too dark – the same police officer who had stood on St Isaac's Bridge at the beginning of our story – made his entrance.

'Are you the gentleman who has lost his nose?'

'Yes, that's me.'

'It's been found.'

'What did you say?' cried Major Kovalyov. He could hardly speak for joy. He looked wide-eyed at the police officer, the candle-light flickering on his fat cheeks and thick lips.

'How did you find it?'

'Very strange. We caught it just as it was about to drive off in the Riga stagecoach. Its passport was made out in the name of some civil servant. Strangely enough, I mistook it for a gentleman at first. Fortunately I had my spectacles with me so

I could see it was really a nose. I'm very short-sighted, and if you happen to stand just in front of me, I can only make out your face, but not your nose, or beard, or anything else in fact. My mother-in-law (that's to say, on my *wife's* side) suffers from the same complaint.'

Kovalyov was beside himself.

'Where is it? I'll go right away to claim it.'

'Don't excite yourself, sir. I knew how much you wanted it back, so I've brought it with me. Very strange, but the main culprit in this little affair seems to be that swindler of a barber from Voznesensky Street: he's down at the station now. I've had my eyes on him a long time on suspicion of drunkenness and larceny, and only three days ago he was found stealing a dozen buttons from a shop. You'll find your nose just as it was when you lost it.'

And the police officer dipped into his pocket and pulled out the nose wrapped up in a piece of paper.

'That's it!' cried Kovalyov, 'no mistake! You *must* stay and have a cup of tea.'

'I'd like to, but I'm expected back at the prison... The price of food has rocketed ... My mother-in-law (on my *wife's* side) is living with me, and all the children as well; the eldest boy seems very promising, very bright, but we haven't the money to send him to school ...'

Kovalyov guessed what he was after and took a note from the table and pressed it into the officer's hands. The police officer bowed very low and went out into the street, where Kovalyov could hear him telling some stupid peasant who had driven his cart up on the pavement what he thought of him.

When the police officer had gone, our collegiate assessor felt rather bemused and only after a few minutes did he come to his senses at all, so intense was his joy. He carefully took the nose in his cupped hands and once more subjected it to close scrutiny.

'Yes, that's it, that's it!' Major Kovalyov said, 'and there's the pimple that came up yesterday on the left-hand side.' The Major almost laughed with joy.

But nothing is lasting in this world. Even joy begins to fade after only one minute. Two minutes later, and it is weaker still, until finally it is swallowed up in our everyday, prosaic state of mind, just as a ripple made by a pebble gradually merges with the smooth surface of the water. After some thought Kovalyov concluded that all was not right again yet and there still remained the problem of putting the nose back in place.

'What if it doesn't stick?'

With a feeling of inexpressible horror he rushed to the table, and pulled the mirror nearer, as he was afraid that he might stick the nose on crooked. His hands trembled. With great care and caution he pushed it into place. But oh! the nose just would not stick. He warmed it a little by pressing it to his mouth and breathing on it, and then pressed it again to the smooth space between his cheeks. But try as he might the nose would not stay on.

'Stay on, you fool!' he said. But the nose seemed to be made of wood and fell on to the table with a strange cork-like sound. The Major's face quivered convulsively. 'Perhaps I can graft it,' he said apprehensively. But no matter how many times he tried to put it back, all his efforts were futile.

He called Ivan and told him to fetch the doctor, who happened to live in the same block, in one of the best flats on the first floor.

This doctor was a handsome man with fine whiskers as black as pitch, and a fresh-looking, healthy wife. Every morning he used to eat apples and was terribly meticulous about keeping his mouth clean, spending at least three quarters of an hour rinsing it out every day and using five different varieties of toothbrush. He came right away. When he had asked the Major if he had had this trouble for very long the doctor pushed back Kovalyov's chin and prodded him with his thumb in the spot once occupied by his nose – so sharply that the Major hit the wall very hard with the back of his head. The doctor told him not to worry and made him stand a little way from the wall and lean his head first to the right. Pinching the place where his nose had been the doctor said 'Hm!' Then he ordered him to move his head to the left and produced another 'Hm!' Finally he prodded him again, making Kovalyov's head twitch like a horse having its teeth inspected.

After this examination the doctor shook his head and said: 'It's no good. It's best to stay as you are, otherwise you'll only make it worse. Of course, it's possible to have it stuck on, and I could do this for you quite easily. But I assure you it would look terrible.'

'That's *marvellous*, that is! How can I carry on without a nose?' said Kovalyov. '*Whatever* you do it couldn't look any worse; and God knows, that's bad enough! How can I go around looking like a freak? I mix with nice people. I'm expected at two soirées today. I know nearly all the best people – Mrs Chekhtaryev, a state councillor's wife, Mrs Podtochin, a staff officer's wife ... after the way *she's* behaved I won't have any more to do with *her*, except when I get the police on her trail.' Kovalyov went on pleading: 'Please do me this one favour – isn't there any way? Even if you only get it to hold on, it wouldn't be so bad, and if there were any risk of it falling off, I could keep it there with my hand. I don't dance, which is a help, because any violent movement might make it drop off. And you may rest assured I wouldn't be slow in showing my appreciation – as far as my pocket will allow of course ...'

The doctor then said in a voice which could not be called loud, or even soft, but persuasive and arresting: 'I never practise my art from purely mercenary motives. That is contrary to my code of conduct and all professional ethics. True, I make a charge for private visits, but only so as not to offend patients by refusing to take their money. Of course, I could put your nose back if I wanted to. But I give you my word of honour, if you know what's good for you, it would be far worse if I tried. Let nature take its course. Wash the area as much as you can with cold water and believe me you'll feel just as good as when you had a nose. Now, as far as the nose is concerned, put it in a jar of alcohol; better still, soak it in two tablespoonsful of sour vodka and warmed-up vinegar, and you'll get good money for it. I'll take it myself if you don't want it.'

'No! I wouldn't sell it for anything,' Kovalyov cried desperately. 'I'd rather lose it again.'

'Then I'm sorry,' replied the doctor, bowing himself out. 'I wanted to help you . . . at least I've tried hard enough.'

With these words the doctor made a very dignified exit. Kovalyov did not even look at his face, and felt so dazed that all he could make out were the doctor's snowy-white cuffs sticking out from the sleeves of his black dress-coat.

The very next day he decided – before going to the police – to write to the staff officer's wife to ask her to put back in its proper place what belonged to him without further ado. The letter read as follows:

Dear Mrs Alexandra Grigoryevna,

I cannot understand this strange behaviour on your part. You can be sure, though, that it won't get you anywhere and you certainly won't force me to marry your daughter. Moreover, you can rest assured that, regarding my nose, I am familiar with the whole history of this affair from the very beginning, and I also know that you, and no one else, are the prime instigator. Its sudden detachment from its rightful place, its subsequent flight, its masquerading as a civil servant and then its re-appearance in its natural state, are nothing else than the result of black magic carried out by yourself or by those practising the same very honourable art. I consider it my duty to warn you that if the above-mentioned nose is not back in its proper place by today, then I shall be compelled to ask for the law's protection.

I remain, dear Madam,

Your very faithful servant,
Platon Kovalyov.

Dear Mr Kovalyov!

I was simply staggered by your letter. To be honest, I never expected anything of this kind from you, particularly those remarks which are quite uncalled-for. I would have you know I have never received that civil servant mentioned by you in my house, whether disguised or not. True, Philip Ivanovich Potanchikov used to call. Although he wanted to ask for my daughter's hand, and despite the fact that he was a very sober, respectable and learned gentleman, I never gave him any cause for hope. And then you go on to mention your nose. If by this you mean to say I wanted to make you look foolish,* that is, to put you off with a formal refusal, then all I can say is that I am very surprised that you can talk like this, as you know well enough my feelings on the matter are quite different. And if you care to make an official proposal to my daughter, I will gladly give my consent, for this has always been my dearest wish, and in this hope I remain at your disposal.

Yours sincerely,
Alexandra Podtochin.

'No,' said Kovalyov when he had read the letter. 'She's not to blame. Impossible! A guilty person could never write a letter like that.' The collegiate assessor knew what he was talking about in this case as he had been sent to the Caucasus several times to carry out legal inquiries. 'How on earth did this happen then? It's impossible to make head or tail of it!' he said, letting his arms drop to his side.

Meanwhile rumours about the strange occurrence had spread throughout the capital, not, need we say, without a few embellishments. At the time everyone seemed very pre-occupied with the supernatural: only a short time before, some experiments in magnetism had been all the rage. Besides, the story of the dancing chairs in Konúshenny Street† was still

*Russian is rich in idioms referring to the nose, most of which have a derogatory meaning, e.g. to make a fool of, etc. (Trans.)

†An entry in Pushkin's diary for 17 December 1833 mentions furniture jumping about in one of the houses attached to the Royal Stables. In 1832 a certain lady called Tatarinova was exiled from St Petersburg for deceiving people into thinking she could will objects to move. (Trans.)

fresh in people's minds, so no one was particularly surprised to hear about Collegiate Assessor Kovalyov's nose taking a regular stroll along the Nevsky Avenue at exactly three o'clock every afternoon. Every day crowds of inquisitive people flocked there. Someone said they had seen the nose in Junker's Store and this produced such a crush outside that the police had to be called.

One fairly respectable-looking, bewhiskered character, who sold stale cakes outside the theatre, knocked together some solid-looking wooden benches, and hired them out at eighty kopecks a time for people to stand on.

One retired colonel left home especially early one morning and after a great struggle managed to barge his way through to the front. But to his great annoyance, instead of a nose in the shop window, all he could see was an ordinary woollen jersey and a lithograph showing a girl adjusting her stocking while a dandy with a small beard and cutaway waistcoat peered out at her from behind a tree – a picture which had hung there in that identical spot for more than ten years. He left feeling very cross and was heard to say: 'Misleading the public with such ridiculous and far-fetched stories shouldn't be allowed.'

Afterwards it was rumoured that Major Kovalyov's nose was no longer to be seen strolling along the Nevsky Avenue but was in the habit of walking in Tavrichesky Park, and that it had been doing this for a long time. When Khozrov-Mirza* lived there, he was astonished at this freak of nature. Some of the students from the College of Surgeons went to have a look. One well-known, very respectable lady wrote specially to the head park-keeper, asking him to show her children this very rare phenomenon and, if possible, give them an instructive and edifying commentary at the same time.

*A Persian prince who had come with official apologies for the murder of the famous playwright A. S. Griboyedov, in Tehran, in 1829. (Griboyedov had gone to Tehran to negotiate with the Shah regarding the Peace of Turkmenchai.) (Trans.)

These events came as a blessing to those socialites (indispensable for any successful party) who loved amusing the ladies and whose stock of stories was completely exhausted at the time.

A few respectable and high-minded citizens were very upset. One indignant gentleman said that he was at a loss to understand how such absurd cock-and-bull stories could gain currency in the present enlightened century, and that the complete indifference shown by the authorities was past comprehension. Clearly this gentleman was the type who likes to make the government responsible for everything, even their daily quarrels with their wives. And afterwards . . . but here again the whole incident becomes enveloped in mist and what happened later remains a complete mystery.

3

This world is full of the most outrageous nonsense. Sometimes things happen which you would hardly think possible: that very same nose, which had paraded itself as a state councillor and created such an uproar in the city, suddenly turned up, as if nothing had happened, plonk where it had been before, i.e. right between Major Kovalyov's two cheeks. This was on 7 April. He woke up and happened to glance at the mirror – there was his nose! He grabbed it with his hand to make sure – but there was no doubt this time. 'Aha!' cried Kovalyov, and if Ivan hadn't come in at that very moment, he would have joyfully danced a trepak round the room in his bare feet.

He ordered some soap and water, and as he washed himself looked into the mirror again: the nose was there. He had another look as he dried himself – yes, the nose was still there!

'Look, Ivan, I think I've got a pimple on my nose.'

Kovalyov thought: 'God, supposing he replies: "Not only is there no pimple, but no nose either!"' But Ivan answered: 'Your nose is quite all right, sir, I can't see any pimple.'

'Thank God for that,' the Major said to himself and clicked his fingers.

At this moment Ivan Yakovlevich the barber poked his head round the corner, but timidly this time, like a cat which had just been beaten for stealing fat.

'Before you start, are your hands clean?' Kovalyov shouted from the other side of the room.

'Perfectly clean.'

'You're lying.'

'On my life, sir, they're clean!'

'Hm, let's have a look then!'

Kovalyov sat down. Ivan Yakovlevich covered him with a towel and in a twinkling had transformed his whole beard and part of his cheeks into the kind of cream served up at merchants' birthday parties.

'Well, I'll be damned,' Ivan Yakovlevich muttered to himself, staring at the nose. He bent Kovalyov's head to one side and looked at him from a different angle. 'That's *it* all right! You'd never credit it . . .' he continued and contemplated the nose for a long time. Finally, ever so gently, with a delicacy that the reader can best imagine, he lifted two fingers to hold the nose by its tip. This was how Ivan Yakovlevich normally shaved his customers.

'Come on now, and mind my nose!' shouted Kovalyov. Ivan Yakovlevich let his arms fall to his side and stood there more frightened and embarrassed than he had ever been in his life. At last he started tickling Kovalyov carefully under the chin with his razor. And although with only his olfactory organ to hold on to without any other means of support made shaving very awkward, by planting his rough, wrinkled thumb on his cheek and lower gum (in this way gaining some sort of leverage) he managed to shave him.

When everything was ready, Kovalyov rushed to get dressed and took a cab straight to the café. He had hardly got inside before he shouted, 'Waiter, a cup of chocolate,' and went straight up to the mirror. Yes, his nose was there! Gaily he turned round, screwed up his eyes and looked superciliously at two soldiers, one of whom had a nose no bigger than a *waistcoat* button. Then he went off to the ministerial department where he was petitioning for a vice-governorship. (Failing this he was going to try for an administrative post.) As he crossed the entrance hall he had another look in the mirror: his nose was still there!

Then he went to see another collegiate assessor (or Major), a great wag whose sly digs Kovalyov used to counter by saying: 'I'm used to your quips by now, you old niggler!'

On the way he thought: 'If the Major doesn't split his sides when he sees me, that's a sure sign everything is in its proper place.' But the collegiate assessor did not pass any remarks. 'That's all right then, dammit!' thought Kovalyov. In the street he met Mrs Podtochin, the staff officer's wife, who was with her daughter, and they replied to his bow with delighted exclamations: clearly, he had suffered no lasting injury. He had a long chat with them, made a point of taking out his snuff-box, and stood there for ages ostentatiously stuffing both nostrils as he murmured to himself: 'That'll teach you, you old hens! And I'm not going to marry your daughter, simply *par amour*, as they say! If you *don't* mind!'

And from that time onwards Major Kovalyov was able to stroll along the Nevsky Avenue, visit the theatre, in fact go everywhere as though absolutely nothing had happened. And, as though absolutely nothing *had* happened, his nose stayed in the middle of his face and showed no signs of wandering off. After that he was in perpetual high spirits, always smiling, chasing all the pretty girls, and on one occasion even stopping at a small shop in the Gostiny Dvor* to buy ribbon for some medal, no one knows why, as he did not belong to any order of knighthood.

*The same shopping arcade substituted by the censorship for Kazan Cathedral in the original version. It was built in the eighteenth century and opened off the Nevsky Avenue. (Trans.)

And all this took place in the northern capital of our vast empire! Only now, after much reflection, can we see that there is a great deal that is very far-fetched in this story. Apart from the fact that it's *highly* unlikely for a nose to disappear in such a fantastic way and then reappear in various parts of the town dressed as a state councillor, it is hard to believe that Kovalyov was so ignorant as to think newspapers would accept advertisements about noses. I'm not saying I consider such an advertisement too expensive and a waste of money: that's nonsense, and what's more, I don't think I'm a mercenary person. But it's all very nasty, not quite the thing at all, and it makes me feel very awkward! And, come to think of it, how *did* the nose manage to turn up in a loaf of bread, and how *did* Ivan Yakovlevich...? No, I don't understand it, not one bit! But the strangest, most incredible thing of all is that authors should write about such things. That, I confess, is beyond my comprehension. It's just ... no, no, I don't understand it at all! Firstly, it's no use to the country whatsoever; secondly, it's no use ... I simply don't know *what* one can make of it ... However, when all is said and done, one can concede this point or the other and perhaps you can even find ... well then you won't find much that *isn't* on the absurd side, will you?

And yet, if you stop to think for a moment, there's a grain of truth in it. Whatever you may say, these things do happen – rarely, I admit, but they do happen.

The Overcoat

things he doesn't tell odr –

In one of our government departments . . . but perhaps I had
better not say exactly *which* one. For no one's more touchy
than people in government departments, regiments, chancel-
leries or indeed *any* kind of official body. Nowadays every
private citizen thinks the whole of society is insulted when he
himself is. They say that not so long ago a complaint was
lodged by a District Police Inspector (I cannot remember which
town he came from) and in this he made it quite plain that the
State and all its laws were going to rack and ruin, and that his
own holy name had been taken in vain without any shadow of
doubt. To substantiate his claim he appended as supplementary
evidence an absolutely enormous tome, containing a highly
romantic composition, in which nearly every ten pages a police
commissioner made an appearance, sometimes in a very
drunken state. And so, to avoid any *further* unpleasantness, we
had better call the department in question *a certain department*.

In a certain department, then, there worked *a certain civil
servant*. On no account could he be said to have a memorable
appearance; he was shortish, rather pock-marked, with reddish
hair, and also had weak eyesight, or so it seemed. He had a
small bald patch in front and both cheeks were wrinkled. His
complexion was the sort you find in those who suffer
from piles . . . but there's nothing anyone can do about that:
the Petersburg climate is to blame.

As for his rank in the civil service* (this must be determined
before we go any further) he belonged to the species known

* The civil service was graded into a hierarchy of fourteen ranks,
introduced by Peter the Great. A titular councillor belonged to the
ninth grade. (Trans.)

as perpetual titular councillor, for far too long now, as we all know, mocked and jeered by certain writers with the very commendable habit of attacking those who are in no position to retaliate. His surname was Bashmachkin, which all too plainly was at some time derived from *bashmak*.*

But exactly when and what time of day and how the name originated is a complete mystery. Both his father and his grandfather, and even his brother-in-law and all the other Bashmachkins went around in boots and had them soled only three times a year. His name was Akaky Akakievich. This may appear an odd name to our reader and somewhat far-fetched, but we can assure him that no one went out of his way to find it, and that the way things turned out he just could not have been called *anything* else. This is how it all happened: Akaky Akakievich was born on the night of 22 March, if my memory serves me right. His late mother, the wife of a civil servant and a very fine woman, made all the necessary arrangements for the christening. At the time she was still lying in her bed, facing the door, and on her right stood the godfather, Ivan Ivanovich Yeroshkin, a most excellent gentleman who was a chief clerk in the Senate, and the godmother, Arina Semyonovna Belo-brushkova, the wife of a district police inspector and a woman of the rarest virtue. The mother was offered a choice of three names: Mokkia, Sossia, or Khozdazat, after the martyr. 'Oh no,' his mother thought, 'such awful names they're going in for these days!' To try and please her they turned over a few pages in the calendar† and again three peculiar names popped up: Triphily, Dula and Varakhasy. 'It's sheer punishment sent from above!' the woman muttered. 'What names! For the life of me, I've never seen anything like them. Varadat or Varukh wouldn't be so bad but as for Triphily and Varakhasy!' They turned over yet another page and found Pavsikakhy and

* *bashmak* – shoe.

† The Orthodox Church calendar, containing a large number of saints' days, and their names. (Trans.)

Vakhtisy. 'Well, it's plain enough that this is fate. So we'd better call him after his father. He was an Akaky, so let's call his son Akaky as well.' And that was how he became Akaky Akakievich. The child was christened and during the ceremony he burst into tears and made such a face it was plain that he knew there and then that he was fated to be a titular councillor. The reason for all this narrative is to enable our reader to judge for himself that the whole train of events was absolutely predetermined and that for Akaky to have any other name was quite impossible.

Exactly *when* he entered the department, and who was responsible for the appointment, no one can say for sure. No matter how many directors and principals came and went, he was always to be seen in precisely the same place, sitting in exactly the same position, doing exactly the same work – just routine copying, pure and simple. Subsequently everyone came to believe that he had come into this world already equipped for his job, complete with uniform and bald patch. No one showed him the least respect in the office. The porters not only remained seated when he went by, but they did not so much as give him a look – as though a common house-fly had just flown across the waiting-room. Some assistant to the head clerk would shove some papers right under his nose, without even so much as saying: 'Please copy this out', or 'Here's an interesting little job', or some pleasant remark you might expect to hear in refined establishments. He would take whatever was put in front of him without looking up to see who had put it there or questioning whether he had any right to do so, his eyes fixed only on his work. He would simply take the documents and immediately start copying them out. The junior clerks laughed and told jokes at his expense – as far as office wit would stretch – telling stories they had made up themselves, even while they were standing right next to him, about his seventy-year-old landlady, for example, who used to beat him, or so they said. They would ask when the wedding

73

was going to be and shower his head with little bits of paper, calling them snow.

But Akaky Akakievich did not make the slightest protest, just as though there were nobody there at all. His work was not even affected and he never copied out one wrong letter in the face of all this annoyance. Only if the jokes became too unbearable – when somebody jogged his elbow, for example, and stopped him from working – would he say: 'Leave me alone, why do you have to torment me?' There was something strange in these words and the way he said them. His voice had a peculiar sound which made you feel sorry for him, so much so that one clerk who was new to the department, and who was about to follow the example of the others and have a good laugh at him, suddenly stopped dead in his tracks, as though transfixed, and from that time onwards saw everything in a different light. Some kind of supernatural power alienated him from his colleagues whom, on first acquaintance, he had taken to be respectable, civilized men. And for a long time afterwards, even during his gayest moments, he would see that stooping figure with a bald patch in front, muttering pathetically: 'Leave me alone, why do you have to torment me?' And in these piercing words he could hear the sound of others: 'I am your brother.' The poor young man would bury his face in his hands and many times later in life shuddered at the thought of how brutal men could be and how the most refined manners and breeding often concealed the most savage coarseness, even, dear God, in someone universally recognized for his honesty and uprightness . . .

One would be hard put to find a man anywhere who so lived for his work. To say he worked with zeal would be an understatement: no, he worked *with love*. In that copying of his he glimpsed a whole varied and pleasant world of his own. One could see the enjoyment on his face. Some letters were his favourites, and whenever he came to write them out he would be beside himself with excitement, softly laughing to

74

himself and winking, willing his pen on with his lips, so you could tell what letter his pen was carefully tracing just by looking at him. Had his rewards been at all commensurate with his enthusiasm, he might perhaps have been promoted to state councillor, much to his own surprise. But as the wags in the office put it, all he got for his labour was a badge in his button-hole and piles on his backside. However, you could not say he was *completely* ignored. One of the directors, a kindly gentleman, who wished to reward him for his long service, once ordered him to be given something rather more important than ordinary copying – the preparation of a report for another department from a completed file. All this entailed was altering the title page and changing a few verbs from the first to the third person. This caused him so much trouble that he broke out in a sweat, kept mopping his brow, and finally said: 'No, you'd better let me stick to plain copying.' After that they left him to go on copying for ever and ever. Apart from this copying nothing else existed as far as he was concerned. He gave no thought at all to his clothes: his uniform was not what you might call green, but a mealy white tinged with red.

His collar was very short and narrow, so that his neck, which could not exactly be called long, appeared to stick out for miles, like those plaster kittens with wagging heads foreign street-pedlars carry around by the dozen. Something was always sure to be sticking to his uniform – a wisp of straw or piece of thread. What is more, he had the strange knack of passing underneath windows just as some rubbish was being emptied and this explained why he was perpetually carrying around scraps of melon rind and similar refuse on his hat. Not once in his life did he notice what was going on in the street he passed down every day, unlike his young colleagues in the Service, who are famous for their hawk-like eyes – eyes so sharp that they can even see whose trouser-strap has come undone on the other side of the pavement, something which never fails to bring a sly grin to their faces. But even if Akaky

Akakievich did happen to notice something, all he ever saw were rows of letters in his own neat, regular handwriting.

Only if a horse's muzzle appeared from out of nowhere, propped itself on his shoulder and fanned his cheek with a gust from its nostrils – only then did he realize he was not in the middle of a sentence but in the middle of the street. As soon as he got home he would sit down at the table, quickly swallow his cabbage soup, and eat some beef and onions, tasting absolutely nothing and gulping everything down, together with whatever the Good Lord happened to provide at the time, flies included. When he saw that his stomach was beginning to swell he would get up from the table, fetch his inkwell and start copying out documents he had brought home with him. If he had no work from the office, he would copy out something else, just for his own personal pleasure – especially if the document in question happened to be remarkable not for its stylistic beauty, but because it was addressed to some newly appointed or important person.

Even at that time of day when the light has completely faded from the grey St Petersburg sky and the whole clerical brotherhood has eaten its fill, according to salary and palate; when everyone has rested from departmental pen-pushing and running around; when his own and everyone else's absolutely indispensable labours have been forgotten – as well as all those other things that restless man sets himself to do of his own free will – sometimes even more than is really necessary; when the civil servant dashes off to enjoy his remaining hours of freedom as much as he can (one showing a more daring spirit by careering off to the theatre; another sauntering down the street to spend his time looking at cheap little hats in the shop windows; another going off to a party to waste his time flattering a pretty girl, the shining light of some small circle of civil servants; while another – and this happens more often than not – goes off to visit a friend from the office living on the third or second floor, in two small rooms with hall and kitchen,

76

and with some pretensions to fashion in the form of a lamp or some little trifle which has cost a great many sacrifices, refusals to invitations to dinner or country outings); in short, at that time of day when all the civil servants have dispersed to their friends' little flats for a game of whist, sipping tea from glasses and nibbling little biscuits, drawing on their long pipes, and giving an account while dealing out the cards of the latest scandal which has wafted down from high society – a Russian can *never* resist stories; or when there is nothing new to talk about, bringing out once again the old anecdote about the Commandant who was told that the tail of the horse in Falconet's statue* of Peter the Great had been cut off; briefly, when everyone was doing his best to amuse himself, Akaky Akakievich did not abandon himself to any such pleasures.

No one could remember ever having seen him at a party. After he had copied to his heart's content he would go to bed, smiling in anticipation of the next day and what God would send him to copy. So passed the uneventful life of a man quite content with his four hundred roubles a year; and this life might have continued to pass peacefully until ripe old age had it not been for the various calamities that lie in wait not only for titular councillors, but even privy, state, court and all types of councillor, even those who give advice to no one, nor take it from anyone.

St Petersburg harbours one terrible enemy of all those earning four hundred roubles a year – or thereabouts. This enemy is nothing else than our northern frost, although some people say it is very good for the health. Between eight and nine in the morning, just when the streets are crowded with civil servants on their way to the office, it starts dealing out indiscriminately such sharp nips to noses of every description that the poor clerks just do not know where to put them.

At this time of day, when the foreheads of even important

*This famous statue in St Petersburg (now Leningrad) shows the horse on its hind legs, with its tail as a third support. (Trans.)

officials ache from the frost and tears well up in their eyes, the humbler titular councillors are sometimes quite defenceless. Their only salvation lies in running the length of five or six streets in their thin, wretched little overcoats and then having a really good stamp in the lobby until their faculties and capacity for office work have thawed out. For some time now Akaky Akakievich had been feeling that his back and shoulders had become subject to really vicious onslaughts no matter how fast he tried to sprint the official distance between home and office. At length he began to wonder if his overcoat might not be at fault here. (weren't there some sins in his overcoat!)

After giving it a thorough examination at home he found that in two or three places – to be exact, on the back and round the shoulders – it now resembled coarse cheese-cloth: the material had worn so thin that it was almost transparent and the lining had fallen to pieces.

At this point it should be mentioned that Akaky Akakievich's coat was a standing joke in the office. It had been deprived of the status of overcoat and was called a dressing-gown instead. And there was really something very strange in the way it was made. With the passing of the years the collar had shrunk more and more, as the cloth from it had been used to patch up other parts. This repair work showed no sign of a tailor's hand, and made the coat look baggy and most unsightly. When he realized what was wrong, Akaky Akakievich decided he would have to take the overcoat to Petrovich, a tailor living somewhere on the third floor up some backstairs and who, in spite of being blind in one eye and having pockmarks all over his face, carried on quite a nice little business repairing civil servants' and other gentlemen's trousers and frock-coats, whenever – it goes without saying – he was sober and was not hatching some plot in that head of his.

Of course, there is not much point in wasting our time describing this tailor, but since it has become the accepted thing to give full details about every single character in a story, there

78

is nothing for it but to take a look at this man Petrovich.

At first he was simply called Grigory and had been a serf belonging to some gentleman or other. People started calling him Petrovich after he had gained his freedom, from which time he began to drink rather heavily on every church holiday – at first only on the most important feast-days, but later on every single holiday marked by a cross in the calendar.* In this respect he was faithful to ancestral tradition, and when he had rows about this with his wife he called her a worldly woman and a German.

As we have now brought his wife up we might as well say something about her. Unfortunately, little is known of her except that she was Petrovich's wife and she wore a bonnet instead of a shawl. Apparently she had nothing to boast about as far as looks were concerned. At least only *guardsmen* were ever known to peep under her bonnet as they tweaked their moustaches and made a curious noise in their throats.

As he made his way up the stairs to Petrovich's (these stairs, to describe them accurately, were running with water and slops, and were saturated with that strong smell of spirit which makes the eyes smart and is a perpetual feature of all backstairs in Petersburg), Akaky Akakievich was already beginning to wonder how much Petrovich would charge and making up his mind not to pay more than two roubles. The door had been left open as his wife had been frying some kind of fish and had made so much smoke in the kitchen that not even the cockroaches were visible.

Mrs Petrovich herself failed to notice Akaky Akakievich as he walked through the kitchen and finally entered a room where Petrovich was squatting on a broad, bare wooden table, his feet crossed under him like a Turkish Pasha. As is customary with tailors, he was working in bare feet. The first thing that

*In the calendar of the Orthodox Church the great festivals were printed in red and the less important saints' days marked with a cross. (Trans.)

struck Akaky was his familiar big toe with its deformed nail, thick and hard as tortoiseshell. A skein of silk and some thread hung round his neck and some old rags lay across his lap. For the past two or three minutes he had been trying to thread a needle without any success, which made him curse the poor light and even the thread itself. He grumbled under his breath: 'Why don't you go through, you swine! You'll be the death of me, you devil!'

Akaky Akakievich was not very pleased at finding Petrovich in such a temper: his real intention had been to place an order with Petrovich after he had been on the bottle, or, as his wife put it, 'after he'd bin swigging that corn brandy again, the old one-eyed devil!'

In this state Petrovich would normally be very amenable, invariably agreeing to any price quite willingly and even concluding the deal by bowing and saying thank you. It is true that afterwards his tearful wife would come in with the same sad story that that husband of hers was drunk again and had not charged enough. But even so, for another kopeck or two the deal was usually settled. But at this moment Petrovich was (or so it seemed) quite sober, and as a result was gruff, intractable and in the right mood for charging the devil's own price. Realizing this, Akaky Akakievich was all for making himself scarce, as the saying goes, but by then it was too late. Petrovich had already screwed up his one eye and was squinting steadily at him. Akaky Akakievich found himself saying:

'Good morning, Petrovich!'

'Good morning to you, sir,' said Petrovich, staring at Akaky's hand to see how much money he had on him.

'I ... er ... came about that ... Petrovich.'

The reader should know that Akaky Akakievich spoke mainly in prepositions, adverbs, and resorted to parts of speech which had no meaning whatsoever. If the subject was particularly complicated he would even leave whole sentences unfinished, so that very often he would begin with: 'That is really exactly what . . .' and then forget to say anything more, convinced that he had said what he wanted to.

'What on earth's that?' Petrovich said, inspecting with his solitary eye every part of Akaky's uniform, beginning with the collar and sleeves, then the back, tails and buttonholes. All of this was very familiar territory, as it was his own work, but every tailor usually carries out this sort of inspection when he has a customer.

'I've er . . . come . . . Petrovich, that overcoat you know, the cloth . . . you see, it's quite strong in other places, only a little dusty. This makes it look old, but in fact it's quite new. Just a bit . . . you know . . . on the back and a little worn on one shoulder, and a bit . . . you know, on the other, that's all. Only a small job . . .'

Petrovich took the 'dressing-gown', laid it out on the table, took a long look at it, shook his head, reached out to the window-sill for his round snuff-box bearing the portrait of some general – exactly which one is hard to say, as someone had poked his finger through the place where his face should have been and it was pasted over with a square piece of paper.

Petrovich took a pinch of snuff, held the coat up to the light, gave it another thorough scrutiny and shook his head again. Then he placed it with the lining upwards, shook his head once more, removed the snuff-box lid with the pasted-over general, filled his nose with snuff, replaced the lid, put the box away somewhere, and finally said: 'No, I can't mend that. It's in a *terrible* state!'

With these words Akaky Akakievich's heart sank.

'And why not, Petrovich?' he asked in the imploring voice of a child. 'It's only a bit worn on the shoulders. Really, you could *easily* patch it up.'

'I've got plenty of patches, plenty,' said Petrovich, 'But I can't sew them all up together. The coat's absolutely rotten. It'll fall to pieces if you so much as touch it with a needle.'

'Well, if it falls to bits you can patch it up again.'

81

'But it's too far gone. There's nothing for the patches to hold on to. You can hardly call it cloth at all. One gust of wind and the whole lot will blow away.'

'But patch it up just a *little*. It can't, hm, be, well . . .'

'I'm afraid it can't be done, sir,' replied Petrovich firmly. 'It's too far gone. You'd be better off if you cut it up for the winter and made some leggings with it, because socks aren't any good in the really cold weather. The Germans invented them as they thought they could make money out of them.' (Petrovich liked to have a dig at Germans.) 'As for the coat, you'll have to have a *new* one, sir.'

The word 'new' made Akaky's eyes cloud over and everything in the room began to swim round. All he could see clearly was the pasted-over face of the general on Petrovich's snuff-box.

'What do you mean, a *new* one?' he said as though in a dream. 'I've got no money.'

'Yes, you'll have to have a new one,' Petrovich said in a cruelly detached voice.

'Well, um, if I had a *new* one, how would, I mean to say, er . . . ?'

'You mean, how much?'

'Yes.'

'You can reckon on three fifty-rouble notes or more,' said Petrovich pressing his lips together dramatically. He had a great liking for strong dramatic effects, and loved producing some remark intended to shock and then watching the expression on the other person's face out of the corner of his eye.

'A hundred and fifty roubles for an overcoat!' poor Akaky shrieked for what was perhaps the first time in his life – he was well known for his low voice.

'Yes, sir,' said Petrovich. 'And even then it wouldn't be much to write home about. If you want a collar made from marten fur and a silk-lined hood then it could set you back as much as two hundred.'

'Petrovich, please,' said Akaky imploringly, not hearing, or at least, trying not to hear Petrovich's 'dramatic' pronouncement, 'just do what you can with it, so I can wear it a little longer.'

'I'm afraid it's no good. It would be sheer waste of time and money,' Petrovich added, and with these words Akaky left, feeling absolutely crushed.

After he had gone Petrovich stayed squatting where he was for some time without continuing his work, his lips pressed together significantly. He felt pleased he had not cheapened himself or the rest of the sartorial profession.

Out in the street Akaky felt as if he were in a dream. 'What a to-do now,' he said to himself. 'I never thought it would turn out like this, for the life of me . . .' And then, after a brief silence, he added: 'Well now then! So this is how it's turned out and I would never have guessed it would end . . .' Whereupon followed a long silence, after which he murmured: 'So that's it! Really, to tell the truth, it's so unexpected that I never would have . . . such a to-do!' When he had said this, instead of going home, he walked straight off in the opposite direction, quite oblivious of what he was doing. On the way a chimney-sweeper brushed up against him and made his shoulder black all over. And then a whole hatful of lime fell on him from the top of a house that was being built. To this he was blind as well; and only when he happened to bump into a policeman who had propped his halberd up and was sprinkling some snuff he had taken from a small horn on to his wart-covered fist did he come to his senses at all, and only then because the policeman said:

'Isn't the pavement wide enough without you having to crawl right up my nose?' перио.

This brought Akaky to his senses and he went off in the direction of home.

Not until he was there did he begin to collect his thoughts and properly assess the situation. He started talking to himself, not in incoherent phrases, but quite rationally and openly, as though he were discussing what had happened with a sensible friend in whom one could confide when it came to matters of the greatest intimacy.

'No, I can see it's impossible to talk to Petrovich now. He's a bit . . . and it looks as if his wife's been knocking him around. I'd better wait until Sunday morning: after he's slept off Saturday night he'll start his squinting again and will be dying for a drink to see him through his hangover. But his wife won't give him any money, so I'll turn up with a kopeck or two. That will soften him up, you know, and my overcoat . . .'

Akaky Akakievich felt greatly comforted by this fine piece of reasoning, and waiting until Sunday came went straight off to Petrovich's. He spotted his wife leaving the house some distance away. Just as he had expected, after Saturday night, Petrovich's eye really was squinting for all it was worth, and there he was, his head drooping towards the floor, and looking very sleepy. All the same, as soon as he realized why Akaky had come, he became wide awake, just as though the devil had given him a sharp kick.

'It's impossible, you'll have to have a new one.' At this point Akaky Akakievich shoved a ten-kopeck piece into his hand.

'Much obliged, sir. I'll have a quick pick-me-up on you,' said Petrovich. 'And I shouldn't worry about that overcoat of yours if I were you. It's no good at all. I'll make you a *marvellous* new one, so let's leave it at that.'

Akaky Akakievich tried to say something about having it repaired, but Petrovich pretended not to hear and said:

'Don't worry, I'll make you a brand-new one, you can depend on me to make a good job of it. And I might even get some silver clasps for the collar, like they're all wearing now.'

Now Akaky Akakievich realized he would *have* to buy a new overcoat and his heart sank. Where was the money coming from? Of course he could just about count on that holiday bonus. But this had been put aside for something else a long time ago. He needed new trousers, and then there was that long-standing debt to be settled with the shoemaker for putting some new tops on his old boots. And there were three shirts he had to order from the seamstress, as well as two items of underwear which cannot decently be mentioned in print. To cut a long story short, all his money was bespoken and he would not have enough even if the Director were so generous as to raise his bonus to forty-five or even fifty roubles. What was left was pure chicken-feed; in terms of *overcoat* finance, the merest drop in the ocean. Also, he knew very well that at times Petrovich would suddenly take it into his head to charge the most fantastic price, so that even his wife could not help saying about him:

'Has he gone out of his mind, the old fool! One day he'll work for next to nothing, and now the devil's making him charge more than he's worth himself!'

He knew very well, however, that Petrovich would take eighty roubles; but the question still remained, where was he to get them from? He could just about scrape half of it together, perhaps a little more. But what about the balance? Before we go into this, the reader should know where the *first* half was coming from.

For every rouble he spent, Akaky Akakievich would put half a kopeck away in a small box, which had a little slot in the lid for dropping money through, and which was kept locked. Every six months he would tot up his savings and change them into silver. He had been doing this for a long time, and over several years had amassed more than forty roubles. So, he had half the money, but what about the rest?

Akaky Akakievich thought and thought, and at last decided he would have to cut down on his day-to-day spending, for a year at least: he would have to stop drinking tea in the evenings; go without a candle; and, if he had copying to do, go to his landlady's room and work there. He would have to step as carefully and lightly as possible over the cobbles in the street – almost on tiptoe – to save the soles of his shoes; avoid taking his personal linen to the laundress as much as possible; and, to make his underclothes last longer, take them off when he got home and only wear his thick cotton dressing-gown – itself an ancient garment and one which time had treated kindly. Frankly, Akaky Akakievich found these privations quite a burden to begin with, but after a while he got used to them. He even trained himself to go without any food at all in the evenings, for his nourishment was *spiritual*, his thoughts always full of that overcoat which one day was to be his. From that time onwards his whole life seemed to have become richer, as though he had married and another human being was by his side. It was as if he was not alone at all but had some pleasant companion who had agreed to tread life's path together with him; and this companion was none other than the overcoat with its thick cotton-wool padding and strong lining, made to last a lifetime. He livened up and, like a man who has set himself a goal, became more determined.

His indecision and uncertainty – in short, the vague and hesitant side of his personality – just disappeared of its own accord. At times a fire shone in his eyes, and even such daring and audacious thoughts as: 'Now, what about having a *marten* collar?' flashed through his mind.

All these reflections very nearly turned his mind. Once he was not far from actually making a *copying mistake*, so that he almost cried out 'Ugh!' and crossed himself. At least once a month he went to Petrovich's to see how the overcoat was getting on and to inquire where was the best place to buy cloth, what colour they should choose, and what price they should pay. Although slightly worried, he always returned home contented, thinking of the day when all the material would be bought and the overcoat finished. Things progressed quicker than he had ever hoped. The Director allowed Akaky Akakievich not forty or forty-five, but a whole *sixty* roubles bonus, which was beyond his wildest expectations. Whether that was because the Director had some premonition that he needed a new overcoat, or whether it was just pure chance, Akaky Akakievich found himself with an extra twenty roubles. And as a result every thing was speeded up. After another two or three months of mild starvation Akaky Akakievich had saved up the eighty roubles. His heart, which usually had a very steady beat, started pounding away. The very next day off he went shopping with Petrovich. They bought some *very* fine material, and no wonder, since they had done nothing but discuss it for the past six months and scarcely a month had gone by without their calling in at all the shops to compare prices. What was more, even Petrovich said you could not buy better cloth anywhere. For the lining they simply chose calico, but calico so strong and of such high quality that, according to Petrovich, it was finer than silk and even had a smarter and glossier look.

They did not buy marten for the collar, because it was really too expensive, but instead they settled on cat fur, the finest cat they could find in the shops and which could easily be mistaken for marten from a distance. In all, Petrovich took two weeks to finish the overcoat as there was so much quilting to be done. Otherwise it would have been ready much sooner. Petrovich charged twelve roubles – anything less was out of the question. He had used silk thread everywhere, with fine double seams, and had gone over them with his teeth afterwards to make different patterns.

It was . . . precisely *which* day it is difficult to say, but without any doubt it was the most triumphant day in Akaky Akakievich's whole life when Petrovich at last delivered the overcoat. He brought it early in the morning, even before Akaky Akakievich had left for the office. The overcoat could not have arrived at a better time, since fairly severe frosts had already set in and were likely to get even worse. Petrovich delivered the overcoat in person – just as a good tailor should. Akaky

Akakievich had never seen him looking so solemn before. He seemed to know full well that his was no mean achievement, and that he had suddenly shown by his own work the gulf separating tailors who only relined or patched up overcoats from those who make new ones, right from the beginning. He took the overcoat out of the large kerchief he had wrapped it in and which he had only just got back from the laundry. Then he folded the kerchief and put it in his pocket ready for use. Then he took the overcoat very proudly in both hands and threw it very deftly round Akaky Akakievich's shoulders. He gave it a sharp tug, smoothed it downwards on the back, and draped it round Akaky Akakievich, leaving some buttons in the front undone. Akaky Akakievich, who was no longer a young man, wanted to try it with his arms in the sleeves. Petrovich helped him, and even this way it was the right size. In short, the overcoat was a perfect fit, without any shadow of doubt. Petrovich did not forget to mention it was only *because* he happened to live in a small backstreet and *because* his workshop had no sign outside, and *because* he had known Akaky Akakievich such a long time, that he had charged him such a low price. If he had gone anywhere along Nevsky Avenue they would have rushed him seventy-five roubles for the labour alone. Akaky Akakievich did not feel like taking Petrovich up on this and in fact was rather intimidated by the large sums Petrovich was so fond of mentioning just to try and impress his clients. He settled up with him, thanked him and went straight off to the office in his new overcoat. Petrovich followed him out into the street, stood there for a long time having a look at the overcoat from some way off, and then deliberately made a small detour up a side street so that he could have a good view of the overcoat from the other side, i.e. coming straight towards him.

Meanwhile Akaky Akakievich continued on his way to the office in the most festive mood. Not one second passed without his being conscious of the new overcoat on his shoulders, and several times he even smiled from inward pleasure. And really the overcoat's advantages were two-fold: firstly, it was warm; secondly, it made him feel good. He did not notice where he was going at all and suddenly found himself at the office. In the lobby he took the overcoat off, carefully examined it all over, and then handed it to the porter for special safe-keeping.

No one knew how the news suddenly got round that Akaky Akakievich had a new overcoat and that his 'dressing-gown' was now no more. The moment he arrived everyone rushed out into the lobby to look at his new acquisition. They so overwhelmed him with congratulations and good wishes that he smiled at first and then he even began to feel quite embarrassed. When they all crowded round him saying they should have a drink on the new overcoat, and insisting that the *very least* he could do was to hold a party for all of them, Akaky Akakievich lost his head completely, not knowing what to do or what to answer or how to escape. Blushing all over, he tried for some considerable time, rather naïvely, to convince them it was not a new overcoat at all but really his old one. In the end one of the civil servants, who was nothing less than an assistant head clerk, and who was clearly anxious to show he was not at all snooty and could hobnob even with his inferiors, said: 'All right then, *I'll* throw a party instead. You're all invited over to my place this evening. It so happens it's my name-day.'

Naturally the others immediately offered the assistant head clerk their congratulations and eagerly accepted the invitation. When Akaky Akakievich tried to talk himself out of it, everyone said it was impolite, in fact quite shameful, and a refusal was out of the question. Later, however, he felt pleased when he remembered that the party would give him the opportunity of going out in his new overcoat that very same evening.

The whole day was like a triumphant holiday for Akaky Akakievich. He went home in the most jubilant mood, took off his coat, hung it up very carefully and stood there for some time admiring the cloth and lining. Then, to compare the two, he brought out his old 'dressing-gown', which by now had completely disintegrated. As he examined it he could not help laughing: what a *fantastic* difference! All through dinner the thought of his old overcoat and its shocking state made him smile. He ate his meal with great relish and afterwards did not do any copying but indulged in the luxury of lying on his bed until it grew dark. Then, without any further delay, he put his clothes on, threw his overcoat over his shoulders and went out into the street. Unfortunately the author cannot say exactly where the civil servant who was giving the party lived: his memory is beginning to let him down badly and everything in Petersburg, every house, every street, has become so blurred and mixed up in his mind that he finds it extremely difficult to say where *anything* is at all. All the same, we do at least know for certain that the civil servant lived in the *best part* of the city, which amounts to saying that he lived miles and miles away from Akaky Akakievich. At first Akaky Akakievich had to pass through some badly lit, deserted streets, but the nearer he got to the civil servant's flat the more lively and crowded they became, and the brighter the lamps shone. More and more people dashed by and he began to meet beautifully dressed ladies, and men with beaver collars. Here there were not so many cheap cabmen* with their wooden basketwork sleighs studded with gilt nails. Instead, there were dashing coachmen with elegant cabs, wearing crimson velvet caps, their sleighs lacquered and covered with bearskins. Carriages with draped boxes simply flew down the streets with their wheels screeching over the snow.

Akaky Akakievich surveyed this scene as though he had never witnessed anything like it in his life. For some years now he had not ventured out at all in the evenings.

* Gogol here uses the word 'Vanka', diminutive of Ivan, the popular term for a cabman with an old, slow horse and ramshackle cab. (Trans.)

Filled with curiosity, he stopped by a brightly lit shop window to look at a painting of a pretty girl who was taking off her shoe and showing her entire leg, which was not at all bad-looking, while behind her a gentleman with side-whiskers and a fine goatee was poking his head round the door of an adjoining room. Akaky Akakievich shook his head and smiled, then went on his way. Why did he smile? Perhaps because this was something he had never set eyes on before, but for which, nonetheless, each one of us has some instinctive feeling. Or perhaps, like many other civil servants he thought: 'Oh, those Frenchmen! Of course, if they happen to fancy something, then really, I mean to say, to be exact, something . . .' Perhaps he was not thinking this at all, for it is impossible to probe deep into a man's soul and discover all his thoughts. Finally he arrived at the assistant head clerk's flat. This assistant head clerk lived in the grand style: a lamp shone on the staircase, and the flat was on the first floor.

As he entered the hall Akaky Akakievich saw row upon row of galoshes. Among them, in the middle of the room, stood a samovar, hissing as it sent out clouds of steam. The walls were covered with overcoats and cloaks; some of them even had beaver collars or velvet lapels. From the other side of the wall he could hear the buzzing of voices, which suddenly became loud and clear when the door opened and there emerged a footman carrying a tray laden with empty glasses, a jug of cream and a basketful of biscuits. There was no doubt at all that the clerks had been there a long time and had already drunk their first cup of tea.

When Akaky Akakievich had hung up his overcoat himself he went in and was struck all at once by the sight of candles, civil servants, pipes and card tables. His ears were filled with the blurred sound of little snatches of conversation coming from all over the room and the noise of chairs being shifted backwards and forwards. He stood very awkwardly in the middle of the room, looking around and trying to think what to do. But they had already spotted him and greeted him with loud shouts, everyone immediately crowding into the hall to have another look at the overcoat. Although he was somewhat overwhelmed by this reception, since he was a rather simple-minded and ingenuous person, he could not help feeling glad at the praises showered on his overcoat. And then, it goes without saying, they abandoned him, overcoat included, and turned their attention to the customary whist tables. All the noise and conversation and crowds of people – this was a completely new world for Akaky Akakievich. He simply did not know what to do, where to put his hands or feet or any other part of himself. Finally he took a seat near the card-players, looking at the cards, and examining first one player's face, then another's. In no time at all he started yawning and began to feel bored, especially as it was long after his usual bedtime.

He tried to take leave of his host, but everyone insisted on his staying to toast the new overcoat with a glassful of champagne. About an hour later supper was served. This consisted of mixed salad, cold veal, meat pasties, pastries and champagne. They made Akaky Akakievich drink two glasses, after which everything seemed a lot merrier, although he still could not forget that it was already midnight and that he should have left ages ago.

So that his host should not stop him on the way out, he crept silently from the room, found his overcoat in the hall (much to his regret it was lying on the floor), shook it to remove every trace of fluff, put it over his shoulders and went down the stairs into the street.

Outside it was still lit-up. A few small shops, which house-serfs and different kinds of people use as clubs at all hours of the day were open. Those which were closed had broad beams of light coming from chinks right the way down their doors, showing that there were still people talking inside, most probably maids and menservants who had not finished exchanging the latest gossip, leaving their masters completely in the dark as to where they had got to. Akaky Akakievich walked along in high spirits, and once, heavens know why, very nearly gave chase to some lady who flashed by like lightning, every part of her body showing an extraordinary mobility. However, he stopped in his tracks and continued at his previous leisurely pace, amazed at himself for breaking into that inexplicable trot. Soon there stretched before him those same empty streets which looked forbidding enough even in the daytime, let alone at night. Now they looked even more lonely and deserted. The street lamps thinned out more and more – the local council was stingy with its oil in this part of the town. Next he began to pass by wooden houses and fences. Not a soul anywhere, nothing but the snow gleaming in the streets and the cheerless dark shapes of low-built huts which, with their shutters closed, seemed to be asleep. He was now quite near the spot where the street was interrupted by an endless square with the houses barely visible on the other side: a terrifying desert. In the distance, God knows where, a light glimmered in a watchman's hut which seemed to be standing on the very edge of the world. At this point Akaky Akakievich's high spirits drooped considerably. As he walked out on to the square, he could not suppress the feeling of dread that welled up inside him, as though he sensed that something evil was going to happen. He looked back, then to both sides: it was as though he was surrounded by a whole ocean. 'No, it's best not to look,' he thought, and continued on his way with his eyes shut. When at last he opened them to see how much further he had to go he suddenly saw two men with moustaches right in front of him, although it was too dark to make them out exactly. His eyes misted over and his heart started pounding.

'Aha, that's *my* overcoat all right,' one of them said in a thunderous voice, grabbing him by the collar. Akaky Akakievich was about to shout for help, but the other man stuck a fist the size of a clerk's head right in his face and said:

93

'Just one squeak out of you!' All Akaky Akakievich knew was that they pulled his coat off and shoved a knee into him, making him fall backwards in the snow, after which he knew nothing more. A few minutes later he came to and managed to stand up, but by then there was no one to be seen. All he knew was that he was freezing and that his overcoat had gone, and he started shouting. But his voice would not carry across the vast square. Not once did he stop shouting as he ran desperately across the square towards a sentry box where a policeman stood propped up on his halberd looking rather intrigued as to who the devil was shouting and running towards him. When he had reached the policeman Akaky Akakievich (in between breathless gasps) shouted accusingly that he had been asleep, that he was neglecting his duty and could not even see when a man was being robbed under his very nose. The policeman replied that he had seen nothing, except for two men who had stopped him in the middle of the square and whom he had taken for his friends; and that instead of letting off steam he would be better advised to go the very next day to see the Police Inspector, who would get his overcoat back for him. Akaky Akakievich ran off home in the most shocking state: his hair – there was still some growing around the temples and the back of his head – was terribly dishevelled. His chest, his trousers, and his sides were covered with snow. When his old landlady heard a terrifying knocking at the door she leaped out of bed and rushed downstairs with only one shoe on, clutching her nightdress to her bosom out of modesty. But when she opened the door and saw the state Akaky Akakievich was in, she shrank backwards. After he had told her what had happened she clasped her hands in despair and told him to go straight to the District Police Superintendent, as the local officer was sure to try and put one over on him, make all kinds of promises and lead him right up the garden path. The best thing was to go direct to the Superintendent himself, whom she actually happened to know, as Anna, the

Finnish girl who used to cook for her, was now a nanny at the Superintendents house. She often saw him go past the houses and every Sunday he went to church, smiled at everyone as he prayed and to all intents and purposes was a thoroughly nice man. Akaky Akakievich listened to this advice and crept sadly up to his room. What sort of night he spent can best be judged by those who are able to put themselves in someone else's place. Early next morning he went to the Superintendent's house but was told that he was asleep. He returned at ten o'clock, but was informed that he was still asleep. He came back at eleven, and was told that he had gone out. When he turned up once again round about lunchtime, the clerks in the entrance hall would not let him through on any account, unless he told them first what his business was, why he had come, and what had happened. So in the end Akaky Akakievich, for the first time in his life, stood up for himself and told them in no uncertain terms that he wanted to see the Superintendent *in person*, that they dare not turn him away since he had come from a government department, and that they would know all about it if he made a complaint. The clerks did not have the nerve to argue and one of them went to fetch the Superintendent who reacted extremely strangely to the robbery. Instead of sticking to the main point of the story, he started cross-examining Akaky Akakievich with such questions as: 'What was he doing out so late?' or 'Had he been visiting a brothel?', which left Akaky feeling very embarrassed, and he went away completely in the dark as to whether they were going to take any action or not. The whole of that day he stayed away from the office – for the first time in his life.

The next morning he arrived looking very pale and wearing his old dressing-gown, which was in an even more pathetic state.

The story of the stolen overcoat touched many of the clerks, although a few of them could not refrain from laughing at Akaky Akakievich even then. There and then they decided to make a collection, but all they raised was a miserable little sum since, apart from any *extra* expense, they had nearly exhausted all their funds subscribing to a new portrait of the Director as well as to some book or other recommended by one of the heads of department – who happened to be a friend of the author. So they collected next to nothing.

One of them, who was deeply moved, decided he could at least help Akaky Akakievich with some good advice. He told him not to go to the local police officer, since although that gentleman might well recover his overcoat somehow or other in the hope of receiving a commendation from his superiors, Akaky did not have a chance of getting it out of the police station without the necessary legal proof that the overcoat was really his. The best plan was to apply to a certain *Important Person*, and this same Important Person, by writing to and contacting the proper people, would get things moving much faster. There was nothing else for it, so Akaky Akakievich decided to go and see this Important Person.

What exactly this Important Person did and what position he held remains a mystery to this day. All we need say is that this Important Person had become important only a short while before, and that until then he had been an *unimportant* person. However, even now his position was not considered very important if compared with others which were still more important. But you will always come across a certain class of people who consider something unimportant which for other people is in fact important. However, he tried all manners and means of buttressing his importance. For example, he was responsible for introducing the rule that all low-ranking civil servants should be waiting to meet him on the stairs when he arrived at the office; that no one, on any account, could walk straight into his office; and that everything must be dealt with in the *strictest* order of priority: the collegiate registrar was to report to the provincial secretary who in turn was to report to the titular councillor (or whoever it was he *had* to report to) so that in this way the matter reached him according to the prescribed procedure. In this Holy Russia of ours everything is infected by a mania for imitation, and everyone apes his superior. I have even heard say that when a certain titular councillor was appointed head of some minor government department he immediately partitioned off a section of his office into a special room for himself, an 'audience chamber' as he called it, and made two ushers in uniforms with red collars and gold braid stand outside to open the doors for visitors – even though you would have a job getting an ordinary writing desk into this so-called chamber.

This Important Person's routine was very imposing and impressive, but nonetheless simple. The whole basis of his system was strict discipline. 'Discipline, discipline, and ... discipline' he used to say, usually looking very solemnly into the face of the person he was addressing when he had repeated this word for the third time. However, there was really no good reason for this strict discipline, since the ten civil servants or so who made up the whole administrative machinery of his department were all duly terrified of him anyway. If they saw him coming from some way off they would stop what they were doing and stand to attention while the Director went through the office. His normal everyday conversation with his subordinates simply *reeked* of discipline and consisted almost entirely of three phrases: 'How dare you? Do you know who you're talking to? Do you realize who's standing before you?'

However, he was quite a good man at heart, pleasant to his colleagues and helpful. But his promotion to general's rank had completely turned his head; he became all mixed up, somehow went off the rails, and just could not cope any more. If he happened to be with someone of equal rank, then he was quite a normal person, very decent in fact and indeed far from stupid in many respects.

But put him with people only one rank lower, and he was really at sea. He would not say a single word, and one felt sorry to see him in such a predicament, all the more so as even *he* felt that he could have been spending the time far more enjoyably.

One could read this craving for interesting company and conversation in his eyes, but he was always inhibited by the thought: would this be going too far for someone in his position, would this be showing too much familiarity and therefore rather damaging to his status? For these reasons he would remain perpetually silent, producing a few monosyllables from time to time, and as a result acquired the reputation of being a terrible bore. This was the Important Person our Akaky Akakievich went to consult, and he appeared at the worst possible moment – most inopportune as far as *he* was concerned – but most opportune for the Important Person. The Important Person was in his office having a very animated talk with an old childhood friend who had just arrived in Petersburg and whom he had not seen for a few years.

At this moment the arrival of a certain Bashmachkin was announced. 'Who's he?' he asked abruptly and was told, 'Some clerk or other.' 'Ah, let him wait, I can't see him just now,' the Important Person replied. Here we should say that the Important Person told a complete lie: he had plenty of time, he had long since said all he wanted to his friend, and for some considerable time their conversation had been punctuated by very long silences broken only by their slapping each other on the thigh and saying:

'Quite so, Ivan Abramovich!' and 'Well yes, Stepan Varlamovich!'

Even so, he still ordered the clerk to wait, just to show his old friend (who had left the Service a fair time before and was now nicely settled in his country house) how long he could keep clerks standing about in his waiting-room. When they really had said all that was to be said, or rather, had sat there in the very comfortable easy chairs to their heart's content without saying a single word to each other, puffing away at their cigars, the Important Person suddenly remembered and told his secretary, who was standing by the door with a pile of papers in his hands: 'Ah yes now, I think there's some clerk or other waiting out there. Tell him to come in.' One look at the timid Akaky Akakievich in his ancient uniform and he suddenly turned towards him and said: 'What do *you* want?' in that brusque and commanding voice he had been practising especially, when he was alone in his room, in front of a mirror, a whole week before his present appointment and promotion to general's rank.

Long before this Akaky Akakievich had been experiencing that feeling of awe which it was proper and necessary for him to experience, and now, somewhat taken aback, he tried to explain, as far as his tongue would allow him and with an even greater admixture than ever before of 'wells' and 'that is to says', that his overcoat was a new one, that he had been robbed in the most barbarous manner, that he had come to ask the Important Person's help, so that through his influence, or by doing this or that, by writing to the Chief of Police or someone else (whoever it might be), the Important Person might get his overcoat back for him.

Heaven knows why, but the general found this approach rather too familiar.

'What do you mean by this, sir?' he snapped again. 'Are you unaware of the correct procedure? Where do you think you are? Don't you know how things are conducted here? It's high time you knew that first of all your application must be handed in at the main office, then taken to the chief clerk, then to the departmental director, then to my secretary, who *then* submits it to me for consideration . . .'

'But Your Excellency,' said Akaky Akakievich, trying to summon up the small handful of courage he possessed, and feeling at the same time that the sweat was pouring off him, 'I took the liberty of disturbing Your Excellency because, well, secretaries, you know, are a rather unreliable lot . . .'

'What, what, what?' cried the Important Person. 'Where did you learn such impudence? Where did you get those ideas from? What rebellious attitude has infected the young men these days?'

Evidently the Important Person did not notice that Akaky Akakievich was well past fifty. Of course, one might call him a young man, relatively speaking; that is, if you compared him with someone of seventy.

'Do you realize who you're talking to? Do you know who is standing before you? Do you understand, I ask you, do you understand? I'm asking you a question!'

At this point he stamped his foot and raised his voice to such a pitch that Akaky Akakievich was not the only one to be scared out of his wits. Akaky Akakievich almost fainted. He reeled forward, his body shook all over and he could hardly stand on his feet. If the porters had not rushed to his assistance he would have fallen flat on the floor. He was carried out almost lifeless. The Important Person, very satisfied that the effect he had produced exceeded even *his* wildest expectations, and absolutely delighted that a few words from him could deprive a man of his senses, peeped at his friend out of the corner of one eye to see what impression he had made. He was not exactly displeased to see that his friend was quite bewildered and was even beginning to show unmistakable signs of fear himself.

Akaky Akakievich remembered nothing about going down the stairs and out into the street. His hands and feet had gone dead. Never in his life had he received such a savage dressing-down from a general – and what is more, a general from another department.

He continually stumbled off the pavement as he struggled on with his mouth wide open in the face of a raging blizzard that whistled down the street. As it normally does in St Petersburg the wind was blowing from all four corners of the earth and from every single side-street. In a twinkling his throat was inflamed and when he finally dragged himself home he was unable to say one word. He put himself to bed and broke out all over in swellings. That is what a 'proper and necessary' dressing-down can sometimes do for you!

The next day he had a high fever. Thanks to the generous assistance of the Petersburg climate the illness made much speedier progress than one might have expected, and when the doctor arrived and felt his pulse, all he could prescribe was a poultice – and only then for the simple reason that he did not wish his patient to be deprived of the salutary benefits of medical aid. However, he *did* advance the diagnosis that Akaky Akakievich would not last another day and a half, no doubt about that, and then: *kaput*. After which he turned to the landlady and said:

'Now, don't waste any time and order a pine coffin right away, as he won't be able to afford oak.'

Whether Akaky Akakievich heard these fateful words – and if he did hear them, whether they shocked him into some feeling of regret for his wretched life – no one has the slightest idea, since he was feverish and delirious the whole time. Strange visions, each weirder than the last, paraded endlessly before him: in one he could see Petrovich the tailor and he was begging him to make an overcoat with special traps to catch the thieves that seemed to be swarming under his bed. Every other minute he called out to his landlady to drag one out which had actually crawled under the blankets.

In another he was asking why his old 'dressing-gown' was hanging up there when he had a *new* overcoat. Then he imagined himself standing next to the general and, after being duly and properly reprimanded, saying: 'I'm sorry, Your Excellency.' In the end he started cursing and swearing and let forth such a torrent of terrible obscenities that his good landlady crossed herself, as she had never heard the like from him in all her born days, especially as the curses always seemed to follow right after those 'Your Excellencies'. Later on he began to talk complete gibberish, until it was impossible to understand anything, except that this jumble of words and thoughts always centred on one and the same overcoat. Finally poor Akaky Akakievich gave up the ghost. Neither his room nor what he had in the way of belongings was sealed off,* in the first place, because he had no family, and in the second place, because his worldly possessions did not amount to very much at all: a bundle of goose quills, one quire of white government paper, three pairs of socks, two or three buttons that had come off his trousers, and the 'dressing-gown' with which the reader is already familiar. Whom all this went to, God only knows, and the author of this story confesses that he is not even interested. Akaky Akakievich was carted away and buried. And St Petersburg carried on without its Akaky Akakievich just as though he had never even existed.

So vanished and disappeared for ever a human being whom no one ever thought of protecting, who was dear to no one, in whom no one was the least interested, not even the naturalist who cannot resist sticking a pin in a common fly and examining it under the microscope; a being who endured the mockery of his colleagues without protesting, who went to his grave without any undue fuss, but to whom, nonetheless (although not until his last days) a shining visitor in the form of an over-coat suddenly appeared, brightening his wretched life for one fleeting moment; a being upon whose head disaster had cruelly fallen, just as it falls upon the kings and great ones of this earth . . .

A few days after his death a messenger was sent with instructions for him to report to the office *immediately*: it was the Director's own orders. But the messenger was obliged to return on his own and announced that Akaky would not be

* The police normally sealed off the house or flat of someone dying without any family or heirs. (Trans.)

coming any more. When asked why not he replied: '"Cos 'e's dead, bin dead these four days.' This was how the office got to know about Akaky Akakievich's death, and on the very next day his place was taken by a new clerk, a much taller man whose handwriting was not nearly so upright and indeed had a pronounced slope.

But who would have imagined that this was not the last of Akaky Akakievich, and that he was destined to create quite a stir several days after his death, as though he were trying to make up for a life spent being ignored by everybody? But this is what happened and it provides our miserable story with a totally unexpected, fantastic ending. Rumours suddenly started going round St Petersburg that a ghost in the form of a government clerk had been seen near the Kalinkin Bridge, and even further afield, and that this ghost appeared to be searching for a lost overcoat. To this end it was to be seen ripping all kinds of overcoats from everyone's shoulders, with no regard for rank or title: overcoats made from cat fur, beaver, quilted overcoats, raccoon, fox, bear – in short, overcoats made from every conceivable fur or skin that man has ever used to protect his own hide. One of the clerks from the department saw the ghost with his own eyes and immediately recognized it as Akaky Akakievich. He was so terrified that he ran off as fast as his legs would carry him, with the result he did not manage to have a very good look: all he could make out was someone pointing a menacing finger at him from the distance. Complaints continually poured in from all quarters, not only from titular councillors, but even from such high-ranking officials as privy councillors, who were being subjected to quite nasty colds in the back through this nocturnal ripping off of their overcoats. The police were instructed to run the ghost in, come what may, dead or alive, and to punish it most severely, as an example to others – and in this they very nearly succeeded. To be precise, a policeman, part of whose beat lay along Kirushkin Alley, was on the point of grabbing the ghost by the collar at the very scene of the crime, just as he was about to tear a woollen overcoat from the shoulders of a retired musician who, in his day, used to tootle on the flute. As he seized the ghost by the collar the policeman shouted to two of his friends to come and keep hold of it, just for a minute, while he felt in his boot for his birch-bark snuff-box to revive his nose (which had been slightly frost-bitten six times in his life). But the snuff must have been one of those blends even a ghost could not stand, for the policeman had barely managed to cover his right nostril with a finger and sniff half a handful up the other when the ghost sneezed so violently that they were completely blinded by the spray, all three of them. While they were wiping their eyes the ghost disappeared into thin air, so suddenly that the policemen could not even say for certain if they had ever laid hands on it in the first place. From then on the local police were so scared of ghosts that they were frightened of arresting even the living and would shout instead: 'Hey you, clear off!' – from a safe distance. The clerk's ghost began to appear even far beyond the Kalinkin Bridge, causing no little alarm and apprehension among fainter-hearted citizens. However, we seem to have completely neglected the Important Person, who, in fact, could almost be said to be the *real* reason for the fantastic turn this otherwise authentic story has taken. First of all, to give him his due, we should mention that soon after the departure of our poor shattered Akaky Akakievich the Important Person felt some twinges of regret. Compassion was not something new to him, and, although consciousness of his rank very often stifled them, his heart was not untouched by many generous impulses. As soon as his friend had left the office his thoughts turned to poor Akaky Akakievich.

Almost every day after that he had visions of the pale Akaky Akakievich, for whom an official wigging had been altogether too much. These thoughts began to worry him to such an extent that a week later he decided to send someone round from the office to the flat to ask how he was and if he could be of any help. When the messenger reported that Akaky Akakievich had died suddenly of a fever he was quite stunned. His conscience began troubling him, and all that day he felt off-colour.

Thinking that some light entertainment might help him forget that unpleasant experience he went off to a party given by one of his friends which was attended by quite a respectable crowd. He was particularly pleased to see that everyone there held roughly the same rank as himself, so there was no chance of any embarrassing situations. All this had an amazingly uplifting effect on his state of mind. He unwound completely, chatted very pleasantly, made himself agreeable to everyone, and in short, spent a very pleasant evening. Over dinner he drank one or two glasses of champagne, a wine which, as everyone knows, is not exactly calculated to dampen high spirits. The champagne put him in the mood for introducing several changes in his plans for that evening: he decided not to go straight home, but to call on a lady of his acquaintance, Karolina Ivanovna, who was of German origin and with whom he was on the friendliest terms. Here I should mention that the Important Person was no longer a young man but a good husband and the respected head of a family. His two sons, one of whom already had a job in the Civil Service, and a sweet sixteen-year-old daughter with a pretty little turned-up nose, came every day to kiss his hand and say 'Bonjour, Papa'. His wife, who still retained some of her freshness and had not even lost any of her good looks, allowed him to kiss her hand first, and then kissed his, turning it the other side up. But although the Important Person was thoroughly contented with the affection lavished on him by his family, he still did not think it wrong to have a lady friend in another part of the town. This lady friend was not in the least prettier or younger than his wife, but that is one of the mysteries of this world, and it is not for us to criticize. As I was saying, the Important Person went downstairs, climbed into his sledge and said to the driver:

'To Karolina Ivanovna's', while he wrapped himself snugly in his warm, very luxurious overcoat, revelling in that happy state of mind, so very dear to Russians, when one is thinking about absolutely nothing, but when, nonetheless, thoughts come crowding into one's head of their own accord, each more delightful than the last, and not even requiring one to make the mental effort of conjuring them up or chasing after them. He felt very contented as he recalled, without any undue exertion, all the gayest moments of the party, all the *bons mots* that had aroused loud guffaws in that little circle: some of them he even repeated quietly to himself and found just as funny as before, so that it was not at all surprising that he laughed very heartily. The boisterous wind, however, interfered with his enjoyment at times: blowing up God knows where or why, it cut right into his face, hurling lumps of snow at it, making his collar billow out like a sail, or blowing it back over his head with such supernatural force that he had the devil's own job extricating himself. Suddenly the Important Person felt a violent tug at his collar. Turning round, he saw a smallish man in an old, worn-out uniform, and not without a feeling of horror recognized him as Akaky Akakievich. The clerk's face was as pale as the snow and was just like a dead man's.

The Important Person's terror passed all bounds when the ghost's mouth became twisted, smelling horribly of the grave as it breathed on him and pronounced the following words: 'Ah, at last I've found you! Now I've, er, hm, collared you! It's *your* overcoat I'm after! You didn't care about mine, *and* you couldn't resist giving me a good ticking-off into the bargain! Now hand over *your* overcoat!' The poor Important Person nearly died. However much strength of character he displayed in the office (usually in the presence of his subordinates) – one only had to look at his virile face and bearing to say: '*There*'s a man for you!' – in this situation, like many of his kind who seem heroic at first sight, he was so frightened that he even began to fear (and not without reason) that he was in for a heart attack. He tore off his overcoat as fast as he could, without any help, and then shouted to his driver in a terrified voice: 'Home as fast as you can!'

The driver, recognizing the tone of voice his master used only in moments of crisis – a tone of voice usually accompanied by some much stronger encouragement – just to be on the safe side hunched himself up, flourished his whip and shot off like an arrow.

Not much more than six minutes later the Important Person was already at his front door. He was coatless, terribly pale and frightened out of his wits, and had driven straight home instead of going to Karolina Ivanovna's. Somehow he managed to struggle up to his room and spent a very troubled night, so much so that next morning his daughter said to him over breakfast: 'You look very pale today, Papa.' But Papa did not reply, did not say a single word to anyone about what had happened, where he had been and where he had originally intended going. The encounter had made a deep impression on him. From that time onwards he would seldom say: 'How dare you! Do you realize who is standing before you?' to his subordinates. And if he did have occasion to say this, it was never without first hearing what the accused had to say. But what was more surprising than anything else the ghostly clerk disappeared completely. Obviously the general's overcoat was a perfect fit. At least, there were no more stories about overcoats being torn off people's backs. However, many officious and over-cautious citizens would not be satisfied, insisting the ghost could still be seen in the remoter parts of the city, and in fact a certain police constable from the Kolomna district saw with his own eyes a ghost leaving a house. However, being rather weakly built – once a quite normal-sized, fully mature piglet which came tearing out of a private house knocked him off his feet, to the huge amusement of some cab-drivers who were standing near by, each of whom was made to cough up half a kopeck in snuff-money for his cheek – he simply did not have the nerve to make an arrest, but followed the ghost in the dark until it suddenly stopped, turned round, asked: 'What do *you* want?' and shook its fist at him – a fist the like of which you will never see in the land of the living. The constable replied: 'Nothing', and beat a hasty retreat. This ghost, however, was much taller than the first, had an absolutely enormous moustache and, apparently heading towards the Obukhov Bridge, was swallowed up in the darkness.

How Ivan Ivanovich quarrelled with Ivan Nikiforovich

1: Ivan Ivanovich and Ivan Nikiforovich

YOU should see Ivan Ivanovich's marvellous short fur jacket! It's fantastic! And the quality of the sheepskins! I just can't begin to describe them. All dove-coloured they are, and shot with frosty white! I'll bet you've never seen the like anywhere else. Heavens, take a look at them from the side, especially if Ivan Ivanovich happens to be talking to someone: simply gorge your eyes on them! I just can't go on describing them to you – velvet, silver, fire! Good heavens, by the name of Nikolai the Miracle Worker, why haven't I got a coat like that! He made it before Agafya Fedosyevena went to Kiev. Do you know Agafya Fedosyevena, the woman who bit the assessor's ear off? Ivan Ivanovich is a fine man! You should see his house in Mirgorod! It's completely surrounded by a veranda made of oak pillars with benches all round it.

When the weather gets too hot he throws off his fur jacket and some of his underclothes and relaxes on the balcony in his shirt-sleeves, watching what's going on in the courtyard and the street. And those apples and pears, growing right by his window – just open it and the branches poke right into the room. That's at the front of the house, but then take a look at his garden. What *hasn't* he got!? Plums, cherries, every kind of vegetable, sunflowers, cucumbers, melons, chick-peas, even a threshing floor and a forge.

He's a fine man, Ivan Ivanovich! He loves melons, they're his favourite food. When dinner is over he comes out on to the veranda in his shirt-sleeves and immediately tells Gapka to bring him his two melons. He cuts them himself, collects the seeds in a special piece of paper and starts eating. Then he tells Gapka to bring him a bottle of ink and he writes: 'These melons were eaten on such and such a date.' If he has company he adds: 'So-and-so joined me.' The late judge of Mirgorod always used to admire Ivan Ivanovich's house and it really is very pretty. I like the way it has a number of little lean-to's, so that if you look at it from a distance, all you can see are a series of roofs rising one above the other, making it look like a plateful of pancakes, or better, tree-fungi. The roof is thatched all over with reeds, and a willow, an oak and a couple of apple-trees spread their branches over it. Little windows with carved, white-washed shutters peep out from among the trees and even stick out into the street. He's a fine man, Ivan Ivanovich! Even the commissioner from Poltava knows him. Dorosh Tarasovich Pukhivochka always pops in to see him on his way back from Khorola. And when Father Petr, who lives in Koliberda, has five or six friends round, he always says he knows nobody who carries out his duties as a Christian so well and gets so much out of life as Ivan Ivanovich.

God, how time flies! It's over ten years since his wife died. He never had any children. Gapka has some, and they often run around the courtyard. Ivan Ivanovich is always giving them biscuits, or slices of melon or pears. Gapka has the keys to the storehouses and cellars, but he keeps the key to the large chest in his bedroom and the middle storehouse himself and doesn't like anyone going in there.

Gapka's a healthy girl, with fresh-looking thighs and cheeks and she goes about in a coarse shift.

And he's such a *pious* man. Every Sunday he puts on his fur jacket and goes to church. Once inside, he bows in all directions and usually stands in the choir, singing a very good bass. And the service is no sooner over than Ivan Ivanovich goes rushing off to visit all the poor of the parish.

Perhaps he wouldn't trouble himself with anything so boring if his own inborn goodness didn't urge him on.

'Good morning, you poor thing,' he says when he has found the most badly crippled old woman, with her tattered, patched-up old dress. 'Where are *you* from?'

'From the farm, sir. I've had nothing to eat or drink for three days now, and my own children have driven me out of the house.'

'You poor thing! Why did you come here?'

'To see if I could beg some bread from someone, sir.'

'Hm, so you want some bread?' Ivan Ivanovich will ask.

'What's wrong with that sir? I could eat a *horse*!'

'Hm. I suppose you want some meat as well?'

'I'll be pleased with anything you're kind enough to give me.'

'Hm! So meat's better than bread, is it?'

'You just can't be fussy when you're hungry. Anything's welcome.'

With this the old woman will hold her hand out.

'God be with you,' Ivan Ivanovich replies. 'Well, what are you standing there for? I'm not going to hit you!'

After questioning one or two others in the same way he finally goes home, and either drops in at Ivan Nikiforovich's for a glass of vodka, or calls on the judge or the mayor.

Ivan Ivanovich loves receiving presents. This pleases him more than anything else.

Ivan Nikiforovich is a very fine man as well. He lives next door to Ivan Ivanovich. They are friends the like of whom the world has never seen. Anton Prokofyevich Pupopuz, who still goes around in a brown frock-coat with blue sleeves and dines every Sunday at the judge's, used to say the devil himself tied Ivan Nikiforovich and Ivan Ivanovich together with a rope. Wherever one of them went, the other was always sure to follow.

Ivan Nikiforovich has never been married. Although some people say he has, that is an absolute lie. I know Ivan Nikiforovich very well, and am in a position to say he has never had the slightest intention of getting married. Who's responsible for all these rumours? In the same way it has got round that he was born with a tail. This story is so ridiculous – and indecent and disgusting into the bargain – that I'm sure I needn't start trying to disprove it for the benefit of my enlightened readers, who doubtless know that only witches (and even then very few) have tails, most of them belonging to the female sex rather than the male.

In spite of their great friendship, they are very different in temperament. The best way to find out about their characters is to compare them. Ivan Ivanovich has the gift of being able to make very agreeable conversation. God, you should hear him talk! The sensation can only be compared with the feeling you get when someone runs his hand through your hair or gently passes his finger across your heel. You listen and listen until your head droops. It's pleasant, very pleasant, like a snooze after a swim. Ivan Nikiforovich, on the other hand, is very quiet, but if he *should* come out with anything, then be careful, for his tongue is sharper than any razor. Ivan Ivanovich is on the thin side and tall. Ivan Nikiforovich is a little shorter, but makes up for it in width. Ivan Ivanovich's head is like a radish with the tail pointing downwards; Ivan Nikiforovich's like a radish with the tail sticking up. It's only after *dinner* that Ivan Ivanovich stretches out on the veranda in his shirt-sleeves. Later in the evening he puts his fur jacket on and goes off somewhere – either to the village stores, which he supplies with flour, or into the fields to catch quail. But Ivan Nikiforovich lies out on the porch all day long – it if isn't too hot he turns his back to the sun – and there he stays. In the morning, if he happens to think of it, he will wander round the yard, see to things in the house, and then come back for another rest. In the old days he used to go round to see Ivan Ivanovich. Ivan Ivanovich is an extraordinarily refined gentleman and you will never hear him say a single indecent word – he is the first to take offence if he hears one. Ivan Nikiforovich sometimes forgets himself, which makes Ivan Ivanovich get up and say: 'Enough, enough, Ivan Nikiforovich, You'd better go out in the sunshine if you're going to say such sacrilegious things.'

Ivan Ivanovich is furious if a fly falls into his beetroot soup. He loses his temper completely, throws the plate up in the air, and gives his housekeeper a ticking-off. Ivan Nikiforovich is terribly fond of having a bath, and when the water reaches his neck he has a table and samovar put in the tub, for he loves drinking tea in the cool. Ivan Ivanovich shaves twice a week, Ivan Nikiforovich once. Ivan Ivanovich is very inquisitive, and God help you if you start telling him something and don't finish. If he's dissatisfied with anything, he lets you know right away. It's very hard to tell just from looking at him if Ivan Nikiforovich is angry or not, and if something has pleased him, he certainly does not show it. Ivan Ivanovich is a rather timid person. Ivan Nikiforovich, on the other hand, as the saying goes, has such enormous folds in his trousers that if you inflated them there would be room enough there for the whole farmyard, barn and outbuildings. Ivan Ivanovich has large expressive tobacco-coloured eyes and a mouth rather like the letter I. Ivan Nikiforovich has small, yellowish eyes almost completely lost between bushy eyebrows and puffy cheeks, and a nose like a ripe plum. If Ivan Ivanovich offers you snuff, he will lick the lid of his snuff-box, flip it open with his finger, and hold it out, saying, if he happens to know you: 'I shall esteem it a favour, my dear sir, if you will take some'; if he doesn't know you, he'll say: 'Not having the privilege of knowing your rank, name or patronymic, will you do me the honour of taking some?' Ivan Nikiforovich will plonk the snuff-box right in your hand and all he'll say is: 'Please take some.' Both Ivan Ivanovich and Ivan Nikiforovich detest fleas, and for this reason neither of them will have any truck with a Jewish trader without first buying some of his patent remedies for these insects – and also giving him a good telling-off for practising the Jewish faith.

All in all, despite certain differences, both Ivan Ivanovich and Ivan Nikiforovich are very nice people.

2: In which we learn what Ivan Ivanovich wanted, how the conversation between Ivan Ivanovich and Ivan Nikiforovich arose, and how it was concluded

ONE July morning Ivan Ivanovich was lying on his veranda. It was a hot day and the dry air was rippling in waves. Ivan Ivanovich had already been to the other side of the town to see the haymakers on the farm and ask the peasants he met what they were doing and why. He was terribly tired and had laid down for a rest. Lying there, he looked at his storehouses, his yard, his sheds, and his chickens running around and thought: 'Good Lord, all this belongs to me! I'm not short of anything. Birds, buildings, granaries, everything I fancy. Genuine distilled vodka; pears and plums in the orchard; poppies, cabbages, peas in the kitchen-garden... *What else* do I need? I'd really like to know...!' As he asked himself this profound question he began to reflect, but at the same time his eyes, in their search for new sights, wandered over Ivan Nikiforovich's fence and settled on a curious scene. A fat peasant woman was bringing out some clothes which had been packed away for some time, to air them on the line. Soon an old uniform with threadbare cuffs was stretching out its arms to embrace a woman's brocade jacket. Behind it spread out a court jacket with coats of arms on the buttons and a moth-eaten collar; and he could see some white twill trousers, stained all over, which had once enveloped Ivan Nikiforovich's legs and which would easily fit his fingers now. Other clothes were soon hung out with them, resembling the letter *u*. Next she hung out a blue cossack tunic that Ivan Nikiforovich had had made twenty years ago when he was preparing for the army and had let his whiskers grow. Then, one after another, there were hung out to air a sword that looked like a church spire, the folds of something resembling a grassy green kaftan with brass buttons as big as kopecks, and a waistcoat, trimmed with gold lace and opening wide in front, peeping out from under them. This waistcoat was soon hidden by an old petticoat which had belonged to his dead grandmother, with pockets big enough to hold a water-melon. All these clothes hanging together struck Ivan Ivanovich as very interesting, with the sun's rays falling on a green or blue sleeve, a red cuff, some gold brocade, or playing on the point of a sword and making everything appear rather strange, like some of those Biblical scenes performed by the strolling players who wander round farms. Above all it recalled the scenes where the people crowd together and look at King Herod in his golden crown, or at Anthony with his goat; when a violin is heard, and a gipsy thrums his lips to make them sound like a drum, when the sun sets, and the freshness of a southern night caresses the shoulders and breasts of plump peasant women, without their even noticing it.

Soon an old woman came out of the storeroom, puffing away under the weight of an ancient saddle with ragged stirrups, worn-out leather holsters, and a saddle cloth which had once been red, with gold embroidery and brass discs.

'What a stupid woman!' thought Ivan Ivanovich. 'She'll be bringing out Ivan Nikiforovich and airing *him* next!' And Ivan Ivanovich was not far wrong. Five minutes later Ivan Nikiforovich's baggy nankeen trousers were hoisted into place and took up nearly half the yard. Then she brought out another sword and a rifle.

'What's she up to?' thought Ivan Ivanovich. 'I never knew Ivan Nikiforovich had a rifle. What does he want with that? Whether he uses it or not, it's a *rifle*. A wonderful piece of workmanship. I've wanted one like that for ages. I'd love to get hold of it – I'd have a great time.'

'Hey there, woman!' Ivan Ivanovich shouted, beckoning with his finger.

The old woman came up to the fence.

'What's that you've got there?'

'You've got eyes, haven't you? A rifle.'

'What make?'

'How should I know! If it were mine, I'd know, wouldn't I? But it's the master's.'

Ivan Ivanovich stood up and began examining the rifle all over, completely forgetting to tell the old woman off for hanging it out to air with the sword.

'It must be made of iron,' the old woman said.

'Hm! Iron. I wonder why,' Ivan Ivanovich said to himself. 'Has the master had it long?'

'Maybe.'

'It's a very fine piece!' Ivan Ivanovich continued. 'I'll ask him if I can have it. What can *he* want it for? Perhaps he'll take something in part-exchange. Is the master home?'

'Yes.'

'What's he doing? Having a lie-down?'

'Yes.'

'Good. I'll go and see him.'

Ivan Ivanovich dressed, took his knotty stick which he kept for dogs – in Mirgorod there were more dogs than people in the streets – and set off.

Although Ivan Nikiforovich's yard adjoined Ivan Ivanovich's, so that you could get from one to the other by climbing over a wattle fence, Ivanovich went the long way round, by way of the street. This street led off into an alley which was so narrow that if two carts drawn by a single horse happened to meet they could not pass and had to stay put until they were hauled backwards by their rear wheels in opposite directions.

Pedestrians made their way as best they could, creeping to one side like the flowers and burdock growing along both sides of the fence. Ivan Ivanovich's shed ran along one side of the alley, and along the other were Ivan Nikiforovich's granary, front gates and dovecote.

Ivan Ivanovich went up to the gates and rattled the latch.

This set off a loud barking inside, but when they recognized a familiar face the dogs – all a host of different colours – ran off wagging their tails. Ivan Ivanovich crossed the courtyard with its Indian doves, fed by Ivan Nikiforovich himself, melon rinds, vegetables, broken wheels, barrel hoops, and a small boy in a dirty shirt – altogether the sort of scene dearly beloved by painters! The shadow cast by the clothes strung out along the line covered most of the yard and made it cooler. A peasant woman gave him a welcoming nod and stood there gaping, rooted to the spot. A small porch with its roof supported by two oak columns adorned the front of the house: in the Ukraine this does not give much protection from the sun, which at this time of the year is no laughing matter, soaking the traveller from head to foot in a warm sweat. From this you will appreciate how much Ivan Ivanovich wanted the rifle, as he normally went out only in the evenings because of the tremendous heat.

The room Ivan Ivanovich entered was quite dark, as the shutters were closed. A ray of sunlight shining through a hole in them took on the colours of the rainbow as it struck the opposite wall, reflecting the thatched roofs, the trees, and the clothes hanging outside, and producing a gaily coloured picture – only making everything look different. All this filled the room with a wonderful half-light.

'Good day to you,' said Ivan Ivanovich.

'Ah, how are you, Ivan Ivanovich,' came a voice from the corner. It was only then that Ivan Ivanovich noticed Ivan Nikiforovich lying on a rug spread out on the floor. 'Sorry you caught me in my birthday suit!' (Ivan Nikiforovich had nothing on, not even a nightshirt.)

'Don't worry. So you've been having a rest today, Ivan Nikiforovich?'

'Yes, how about you, Ivan Ivanovich?'

'I've been resting too.'

'But you're up now?'

'Up? For goodness sake! How can anyone sleep so late! I've just been on the farm. You should see the barley! Marvellous! And the hay is tall and soft and golden!'

'Gorpina!' Ivan Nikiforovich shouted. 'Bring some vodka and pastries with sour cream for Ivan Ivanovich.'

'Lovely weather we're having today.'

'How can you say that! It can go to the devil! You just can't escape this heat.'

'You mustn't speak of the devil, Ivan Nikiforovich. You'll remember my words when it's too late: you'll pay for it in the next world if you go on using expressions like that.'

'But why are you so annoyed, Ivan Ivanovich? I haven't laid hands on your mother or father. What's wrong?'

'Forget it, Ivan Nikiforovich!'

'But I didn't *insult* you, Ivan Ivanovich.'

'Strange, the quails don't rise to answer the whistle yet.'

'Think what you like, but I said nothing to cause offence.'

'I don't know why they don't come,' said Ivan Ivanovich, as if he had not heard. 'It's about time they came, but perhaps they're waiting until later.'

'You said the barley's good this year?'

'Marvellous, absolutely marvellous.'

Silence followed. At last Ivan Ivanovich said: 'Why have you hung out all your clothes like that?'

'Well, that stupid woman went and ruined those beautiful clothes, almost new they were. So I'm having them aired. The cloth's still good, and they only need turning a bit to make them fit to wear.'

'One thing rather caught my fancy, Ivan Nikiforovich.'

'What was that?'

'Tell me, do you need that rifle you've hung out to air?' At this point Ivan Ivanovich offered him some snuff. 'Please take some,' he said.

Ivan Nikiforovich rummaged around in his pockets and produced a snuff-box. 'Don't tell me that stupid woman has put the gun out to air. That Jew at Sorochintsy makes very good snuff. I don't know what he puts in it to make it smell so nice. Here, take some and have a chew. Like tansy, isn't it? Please take some.'

'But about that rifle of yours, Ivan Nikiforovich. What are you going to do with it? It can't be any use to you.'

'Why not? I might want to do some shooting.'

'Good God, I'd like to see the day! At the Second Coming, more likely. If I know you, you've never even shot a duck, you're not the type to use a gun. You're too *dignified*. How *can* you chase round the marshes, when at this very moment a certain item of clothing, which is better left unmentioned for propriety's sake, is hanging out to air? No, you need *repose* and *relaxation*.' (I said earlier on that Ivan Ivanovich had a very picturesque turn of phrase when he wanted to be convincing. How he could talk! God, how he could talk!) 'And you should learn to behave *politely*! Please give the rifle to me!'

'Don't be ridiculous. It's a valuable weapon. You won't find one like that anywhere today. I bought it from a Turk when I was about to join the army. And you want me to give it away! Impossible. It's *indispensable*.'

'What do you mean, indispensable?'

'Do you really want to know? Supposing the house were attacked by robbers! I should say it's indispensable! Good heavens, my mind's at rest now and no one can frighten me. And why? Because I know there's a rifle in my storehouse.'

'A fine weapon! But the lock isn't any good, my dear Ivan Nikiforovich.'

'What do you mean, it isn't any good? I can have it mended. All it needs is rubbing down with hemp-oil to stop it going rusty.'

'From what you say, Ivan Nikiforovich, I see you are not *amicably disposed* towards me.'

'How can you say that? You ought to be ashamed of yourself. I let your oxen graze on my pastures and I've never asked any money for it. You always want to use my carts when you go to Poltava, and have I ever refused you? Those children of yours are always climbing over my fence and playing with my dogs, and I've never complained. As long as they don't touch anything I don't mind. Let them enjoy themselves!'

'If you don't want to *give* me the rifle, how about taking something in exchange?'

'And what have you in mind?' As he said this Ivan Nikiforovich leaned on one elbow and looked at Ivan Ivanovich.

'I'll give you my dark-brown sow, the one I feed in the sty. A wonderful sow! You'll see, she'll present you with a litter next year.'

'How *can* you say that, Ivan Ivanovich? What should I do with a pig? Eat it at the devil's own funeral dinner?'

'There, you've said it again, you and your devil – you can't do without him! It's a mortal sin to swear, Ivan Nikiforovich!'

'And what a liberty on your part, Ivan Ivanovich, offering the devil knows what for my rifle! A pig!'

'And why is my pig "the devil knows what"?'

'Why, you can judge for yourself. There's nothing complicated about a rifle, but the devil knows how a pig is going to turn out! If it weren't you speaking to me, I could easily take this as an insult!'

'And have you noticed anything wrong with the sow?'

'Who do you take me for? Don't I know a good sow when I see one? . . .'

'Relax, relax, please! I won't mention it any more. Your rifle can stay and rot in the corner as far as I'm concerned.'

Thereupon silence followed.

'I've heard,' Ivan Ivanovich began, 'that three kings have declared war on the Tsar.'

'Yes, Pyotr Fyodorovich was telling me. What's the reason?'

'I really can't say, Ivan Nikiforovich. I suppose the three kings want to convert us to the Turkish faith.'

'The stupid fools, if that's their game,' said Ivan Nikiforovich, raising his head.

'And now, because of that, the Tsar's declared war on *them*. "No," he told them, "you adopt the *Christian* faith."'

'We'll beat them easily enough, Ivan Ivanovich!'

'Of course we will ... So you don't feel like swapping your rifle, Ivan Nikiforovich?'

'I can't understand a man of your ability talking like a child. I'd be a fool ...'

'Lie down, lie down, and to hell with the rifle. Let it rot! I shan't so much as mention it again.'

At this moment some savouries were brought in.

Ivan Ivanovich drank a glass of vodka and ate a pie filled with sour cream.

'Listen, Ivan Nikiforovich. I'll give you the pig, plus two sacks of oats. You haven't sown any yet, and you'll have to buy some sooner or later this year.'

'Good God, Ivan Ivanovich! It's a waste of time talking to you. Who ever heard of swapping a rifle for two sacks of oats? How about that fur coat of yours!'

'But you're forgetting there's a sow thrown in as well.'

'What! Two sacks of oats and a sow for a rifle?'

'Well, that's fair enough, isn't it?'

'For my *rifle*?'

'That's what I said.'

'Two sacks of oats for a rifle?'

'Not empty sacks, of course, but full of oats. And don't forget the sow.'

'Go and make love to your sow; or go to hell!'

'Temper, temper, now! In the next world they'll stick red hot needles in your tongue for such sacrilegious words! A man needs washing and disinfecting after talking to you.'

'If you don't mind, Ivan Ivanovich, my rifle is no *common* object. In fact it's quite a rarity. What's more, it's very decorative ...'

'You carry on about that rifle like a child with a new toy,' said Ivan Ivanovich, annoyance creeping into his voice. He was really getting angry now.

'And you, Ivan Ivanovich, are a *goose*.'

If Ivan Nikiforovich hadn't used this word there would never have been any quarrel and they would have parted good friends.

But it was not to be. Ivan Ivanovich immediately flared up.

'*What* did you say, Ivan Nikiforovich?' he said, raising his voice.

'I said, you look like a *goose*.'

'How dare you, sir, be so oblivious of the honour and respect my rank and station deserve, and insult me with such a slanderous word.'

'What's slanderous about it, and why are you waving your arms about, Ivan Ivanovich?'

'I repeat, what's happened to your sense of *decency*, that you can go so far as to call me a *goose*?'

'I'd like to spit in your face, Ivan Ivanovich! What on earth are you cackling about?'

Ivan Ivanovich could not control himself any more: his lips trembled, and his mouth changed from its normal 'I' shape and began to look like the letter 'O'. His eyes started blinking in a terrifying way. Ivan Ivanovich had to be thoroughly annoyed to look like this.

'For your information,' Ivan Ivanovich said, 'I don't want to have anything more to do with you.'

'What a shame! Don't worry, I won't lose any sleep over that!' Ivan Nikiforovich answered.

This was a lie: he was really very upset.

'I'll never step inside your house again.'

'Aha!' Ivan Nikiforovich said, as he rose to his feet. He was so furious he just could not think what to do.

'Hey there, woman, boy!'

At this the same fat woman appeared, together with a small

boy wrapped up in a long wide coat. 'Get hold of Ivan Ivanovich and show him the front door!'

'What! You'd do this to a *gentleman*?' shouted Ivan Ivanovich, his feeling of dignity changing to indignation. 'Just you dare! Come on then! I'll flay the living daylights out of you and your stupid master. They won't even find the bodies!' (Ivan Ivanovich used strong language when aroused.)

All together they made a striking picture; Ivan Nikiforovich standing in the middle of the room in his full natural beauty, unadorned; the peasant woman with her mouth wide open and a stupid, terrified look on her face; and Ivan Ivanovich with his arm raised high like a Roman senator. It was a truly great moment, a wonderful sight! And there was only one person to see it – the boy in the immense coat who stood there quietly and picked his nose.

Finally Ivan Ivanovich reached for his hat.

'A fine way to behave, Ivan Nikiforovich. Absolutely wonderful. I'll see you don't forget it in a hurry.'

'Get out! And keep out of my way, or I'll bash your ugly mug in.'

'And that's for you, Ivan Nikiforovich,' Ivan Ivanovich answered, as he made an obscene gesture with two fingers and slammed the door so hard it rattled on its hinges and banged open again.

Ivan Nikiforovich appeared in the doorway and was about to add something more, but Ivan Ivanovich did not stop to turn round and flew through the courtyard.

3: What happened after the quarrel between Ivan Ivanovich and Ivan Nikiforovich

THAT is how two respectable men, the pride and glory of Mirgorod, came to quarrel. And because of what? A stupid trifle, a goose! They refused to see each other again and broke off all relations – yet these were two friends who before had always been thought of as inseparable. Every day Ivan Ivanovich and Ivan Nikiforovich used to send a servant to inquire about the other's health, and they often used to chat to each other from their balconies, saying such pleasant things, it warmed your heart to listen to them. On Sundays they used to set out for church arm-in-arm, Ivan Ivanovich in his light woollen jacket, and Ivan Nikiforovich in his yellowish-brown velveteen Cossack coat.

If Ivan Ivanovich, who had very sharp eyesight, happened to spot a puddle or some refuse in the middle of the street (a very common sight in Mirgorod) before his friend did, then he always used to say: 'Careful, don't step there, it's dirty.' For his part, Ivan Nikiforovich displayed the same touching signs of friendship and wherever he happened to be standing always offered Ivan Ivanovich his snuff-box with the words: 'Do take some please.' And how *well* they ran their estates, these two friends!... When I heard about the quarrel, I was simply thunderstruck. For a long time I just couldn't believe it: Ivan Ivanovich had quarrelled with Ivan Nikiforovich! Such a fine pair! Was there nothing lasting in this world?

When Ivan Ivanovich arrived home he took a long time to calm down. Usually he went to the stables first to see whether the mare was eating her hay (Ivan Ivanovich had a grey mare with a white patch on her forehead – a very fine horse). Then he would go off to feed the turkeys and piglets from his own hands, after which he would retire to his room either to carve wooden plates and dishes (he was as skilful as any professional woodcarver in making things from wood), or he would read some books printed by Lyubya, Garya and Popov (Ivan Ivanovich couldn't remember their titles because one of the kitchen-maids had long ago torn off the top half of the title page when she was playing with the children); or he would have a rest on the veranda.

But now he didn't do any of these things. Instead he gave Gapka a telling-off for lazing around, whereas in fact she was busy carrying barley into the kitchen. He flung his stick at a cock which had come up to the porch for its customary offering; and when the filthy little boy in the torn shirt ran up to him shouting: 'Uncle, uncle, give me some gingerbread,' he threatened him so violently and stamped so hard that the terrified child ran off God knows where.

In the end he thought better of it and busied himself around the house again. He dined very late and it was almost dark when he stretched out on the veranda. A good plate of borshch with pigeons, cooked by Gapka, had completely banished the morning's events from his memory. Once again he took pleasure in surveying his possessions. Finally he looked at the neighbouring courtyard and said to himself: 'I haven't been to Ivan Nikiforovich's today. I think I'll pay him a visit,' whereupon he took his stick and his hat and went out into the street. He had hardly passed through the gates, though, when he remembered the quarrel; he spat and went back. Almost the same thing happened at Ivan Nikiforovich's. Ivan Ivanovich saw a peasant woman step on to the wattle fence, evidently intending to climb across into his courtyard, when he suddenly heard Ivan Nikiforovich shout: 'Come back, come back, don't go in there!' Ivan Ivanovich found this all rather tiresome; and the two worthy gentlemen could easily have made it up the very next day if something that happened in Ivan Nikiforovich's house had not destroyed all hope of reconciliation and poured oil on the hostile fires which were ready to die out.

That very same evening Agafya Fedosyevena came to see Ivan Nikiforovich. She was neither a relative, nor his sister-in-law, nor even his godmother. There was no reason at all why she should visit him, and Ivan Nikiforovich was not exactly pleased when she did. All the same, she was in the habit of coming to stay with him for weeks on end, sometimes even longer, keeping the keys in her possession and taking charge of the whole house. All this Ivan Nikiforovich found very unpleasant, but, surprisingly enough, he obeyed her like a child, and although he sometimes tried to argue with her she always got her way.

I must confess I have no idea how women can grab us by the nose as deftly as they take hold of a teapot handle. Either their hands are adapted for this, or else that is all our noses are fit for. And although Ivan Nikiforovich's nose looked rather like a plum, she would catch hold of it and lead him around like a dog. When she was in the house he could not help changing his routine: he would not lie so long in the sun, and when he did, he would never lie in the nude, but would always wear a shirt and his broad velveteen trousers, although Agafya Fedosyevena never asked him to. On the contrary, she did not like ceremony and when Ivan Nikiforovich felt feverish, she would wash him from head to foot with turpentine and vinegar, with her own hands. Agafya Fedosyevena wore a cap and a coffee-coloured cloak with yellowish flowers, and she had three warts on her nose. She had a figure like a small tub and it was about as difficult to make out where her waist was as trying to see one's own nose without a mirror. Her little legs were shaped like cushions. She loved scandal-mongering, ate boiled beetroot in the mornings, swore like a trooper – and whichever of these activities she happened to be engaged in her expression never altered for a second. This is a gift that normally only *women* are blessed with.

As soon as she arrived everything was turned upside down: 'You mustn't apologize to him, Ivan Nikiforovich, or try and make it up: he wants to ruin you, he's that kind of man! You don't really know him at all.' The wretched woman babbled on and on until, in the end, Ivan Nikiforovich didn't want to know any more about Ivan Ivanovich.

Great changes took place in the house: if a neighbour's dog strayed into the courtyard it was beaten with the first thing that came to hand; children who climbed over the fence came back howling, their shirts lifted up to show where they had been flogged. When Ivan Ivanovich wanted to ask the peasant woman something or other, she replied so obscenely that Ivan Ivanovich, extremely sensitive man that he was, spat on the ground and murmured: 'What a filthy woman! Worse than her master!'

Finally, to add insult to injury, his neighbour built a goose shed just where he used to climb over the fence. This hideous shed was built with diabolical speed – in a single day.

All this filled Ivan Ivanovich with malice and a desire for revenge. However, he did not show any signs of annoyance, despite the fact that the shed actually encroached on his land. But his heart began to beat so fast that he found it very difficult to keep up this outward show of calm. He felt like this for the rest of the day.

Night came ... Oh, if only I were a painter, so that I could portray the wonders of night! I would paint the whole town as it slept; the countless motionless stars looking down on it; the almost visible silence, broken by dogs barking nearby or in the distance; the lovelorn sexton climbing over the fence with the boldness of knights of old; the white walls of the houses caught by moonlight shining even brighter than by day, and the trees overhanging them turning even darker and casting deeper shadows; the flowers and silent grass smelling more fragrant; and the crickets, those restless cavaliers of the night, singing their friendly chirruping songs in unison all over the town. I would paint the black-browed village maiden tossing about on her lonely bed in one of the tiny low-roofed clay cottages, her bosom heaving as she dreamt of some hussar's moustache and spurs, and the moonlight laughing on her cheeks. I would paint the black shadows of bats flitting along the white road and settling on chimney pots blanched in the moonlight. But to paint Ivan Ivanovich as he went out that night, saw in hand, is beyond my powers. His face registered a hundred different expressions.

Ivan Nikiforovich's dogs had not heard yet about the quarrel and, treating him as an old friend, let him go up to the shed, which was supported by four oaken posts. He crept up to the nearest one and started sawing. Because of the noise he was making he kept looking round apprehensively, but his courage returned when he thought of the way he had been insulted. When he had sawn through the first post, he started on another. His eyes seemed to be on fire and he was blinded with terror. Suddenly he cried out loud and went numb all over, for he thought he had seen a ghost, but he quickly recovered when he realized it was a goose sticking its neck out at him. He spat with annoyance and carried on with his work. The second post was sawn through. The shed tottered. His heart started beating so hard when he attacked the third that he had to stop several times. When he had sawn more than half-way through, the shaky building leaned right over. He barely had time to jump back before the whole shed crashed to the ground. Scared out of his wits, he grabbed the saw and ran home, threw himself on his bed and did not even dare to look out of his window to see the terrible results of what he had just done. He imagined Ivan Nikiforovich's entire household – the old woman, Ivan Nikiforovich himself, the boy in the enormous coat – all armed with clubs, and led by Agafya Fedosyevena, coming to smash his house up.

The whole of the next day Ivan Ivanovich was feverish. He had visions of his neighbour revenging himself by burning down his house at the very least. So he ordered Gapka to keep a constant look-out everywhere for dry straw. Finally, he decided to dash straight off to the Mirgorod District Court and file a complaint before Ivan Nikiforovich could take any action. The gist of this complaint will be found in the next chapter.

4: What took place in the Mirgorod District Court

MIRGOROD is a wonderful town! So many different buildings: some with straw roofs, others thatched with reed, some even made of wood! There are streets to right and left, and a fine wattle fence everywhere. Hop vines twine along it, pots hang on it. Behind, sunflowers poke their sun-shaped heads out, poppies blush, fat pumpkins gleam ... Such richness! The wattle fence is always decorated with objects that make it look even more picturesque: women's petticoats and check woollen underclothes, or broad velveteen trousers. Theft or swindling are unknown in Mirgorod and everyone can hang up what he likes. If you walk along to the square, you certainly *must* stop and admire the view: in the middle there is a pond, a really beautiful one, the finest you ever set eyes on! It takes up nearly the whole of the square. Houses and cottages, easily mistaken for haystacks from the distance, stand all around it and wonder at its beauty.

But I am inclined to agree with those who say the courthouse is the finest building. I do not care whether it is made of oak or birch, but, my dear sirs, it has eight windows! All in a row they are, and they look straight on to the square and that watery expanse I have just described, which the mayor calls a lake! It is the only building in Mirgorod painted the colour of granite; all the others are simply whitewashed. It has a wooden roof, which might even have been painted red if the clerks had not flavoured the primer with onion (during a fast of course) and drunk it. As a result the roof did not get painted at all. A porch juts out into the square, and often one can see chickens running about it, for they are fed by careless visitors dropping grains of barley (or anything else they can eat) all over it. It is divided into two sections: one is the courtroom, the other is taken up by the cells. The courtroom section comprises two tidy whitewashed rooms – one of them for clients, and the other housing a table covered all over with ink spots. On this table stands a 'Mirror of Justice'.* There are four oak chairs with high backs, and by the wall stand some iron-bound chests

*A pyramid-shaped glass case showing Peter the Great's Statutes. (Trans.)

containing bundles of documents relating to local libel cases. At this time a pair of wax polished boots stood on one of them.

The court had been sitting since morning. The judge, who was a rather stout man, but thinner than Ivan Nikiforovich, with a kindly face, a greasy dressing-gown, a pipe, and a cup of tea, was having a chat with the clerk of the court. The judge's lips were right underneath his nose, very close to it in fact so he could easily sniff along his upper lip. In fact, this lip of his was as good as a snuff-box, and he always kept some grains of snuff – eventually destined for his nose – scattered all over it.

As I was saying, the judge was chatting with the clerk of the court. A bare-footed girl stood by them with a tray and tea cups.

At the end of the table a secretary was reading out some verdict or other, in such a monotonous and doleful voice that it would have sent any defendant straight off to sleep. The judge himself, no doubt, would have succumbed before anyone else if he had not become involved in a very interesting conversation.

'I made a special point of finding out,' the judge said as he sipped his tea, which was already cold, 'how they manage to sing so well. I had a splendid thrush about two years ago. And what do you think? It suddenly went haywire and began to sing God knows what! As time went on, it got worse and worse: it began to slur its letters, especially ''r'', and its voice became very hoarse – so that I was ready to throw it out! And the cause was really nothing at all! There was a little swelling in its throat – smaller than a pea. All you had to do was prick it with a needle. That's what Zakhar Prokofiev taught me, and if you want to know any more, I'll tell you what happened. I went to see him . . .'

'Shall I read out another verdict, Demyan Demyanovich?' interrupted the secretary, who had stopped reading several minutes before.

'Finished already? That was quick! I didn't hear a word. Where is it? Give it me and I'll sign it. Anything else?'

'There's the case of the Cossack Bokitko and the stolen cow.'

'Good. Read it out! As I was saying, I went to see him . . . I can even remember every single thing we had to eat. With the vodka he served dried sturgeon – wonderful! Not the sturgeon you get here' (as he said this the judge licked his lips and smiled as he sniffed from his permanent snuff-box) 'in Mirgorod. I didn't have any herrings – as you know, they give me heartburn. But I tried some of the caviar. It was excellent, and no mistake! Then I drank some peach vodka, made with real centaury. Then there was saffron vodka, but as you know I don't drink it, though they say it's very good for whetting the appetite and finishing off a meal with afterwards . . . Well, talk of the devil . . .' cried the judge when he saw Ivan Ivanovich enter.

'Good day, gentlemen, I hope you are well,' Ivan Ivanovich said, bowing all round with his usual geniality. Heavens, he really was a great charmer! I have never seen such refinement. He had a very exalted opinion of himself and expected everyone to show him the respect he thought he deserved. The judge himself handed Ivan Ivanovich a chair and his nose inhaled all the snuff resting on his upper lip – always a sign of great pleasure with him.

'What can we give you, Ivan Ivanovich?' he asked. 'A cup of tea perhaps?'

'No, thank you very much,' answered Ivan Ivanovich as he bowed and took a seat.

'Please, just one little cup,' the judge said.

'Really, not at the moment, thanks very much,' Ivan Ivanovich answered, as he stood up, bowed, and sat down again.

'One cup,' repeated the judge.

'Don't bother, please, Demyan Demyanovich.' Ivanovich got up and bowed again.

'A teeny, weeny cup then?'

'All right then, just a small cup!' said Ivan Ivanovich, reaching out for the tray.

Good God, how refined some people can be! It is impossible for anyone to describe the very pleasant impression that such good manners can make.

'Would you care for another cup?'

'No, thank you very much,' Ivan Ivanovich answered, as he put his cup upside down on the tray and got up to say his farewell.

'*Please* have some more, Ivan Ivanovich!'

'I can't stop, thank you very much.' With these words Ivan Ivanovich bowed and sat down again.

'Ivan Ivanovich, I insist you have just one more small cup!'

'No, but I do appreciate your hospitality.' Once again, he got up and bowed – and sat down again.

'Just a small cup, just one more.'

Ivan Ivanovich reached out and took a cup from the tray. Lord, what a man will do to bolster his own dignity!

'Demyan Demyanovich,' said Ivan Ivanovich, draining his cup to the last drop, 'I have come on urgent business. I want to issue a writ.'

Ivan Ivanovich put his cup down and took a sheet of paper from his pocket, which bore an official stamp and had writing all over it. 'It's against my enemy, my *mortal* enemy.'

'Who?'

'Ivan Nikiforovich Dovgochkhun.'

At these words the judge nearly fell off his chair.

'What did you say?' he said, clasping his hands. 'Did you say *you* were taking him to court?'

'Yes, you can see it's me.'

'Well, by all that's holy! *You* are no longer friends with Ivan Nikiforovich, if I heard correctly! It can't be *you* speaking? Repeat what you told me just now. Are you sure there's no one standing behind you and speaking instead?'

'And what's so funny? It makes me sick just to look at him. He has behaved in the most insulting manner and blackened my name.'

'By the Holy Trinity! How can I expect my mother to believe what I say now? Every day, when I've been quarrelling with my sister, the old woman says: "You two behave like animals. If only you followed Ivan Ivanovich's and Ivan Nikiforovich's example. That's what you call real friends, true friendship! Such respectable people!" But tell me what on earth has happened.'

'It's a very delicate matter, Demyan Demyanovich, and I can't tell you in a few words. You'd better have the writ read out.'

'Read it out, Taras Tikhonovich,' said the judge, turning to his secretary.

Taras Tikhonovich took the document and began to read, after he had blown his nose as only secretaries in provincial courthouses know how to – with two fingers.

From a gentleman and landowner of the Mirgorod District, Ivan Pererepenko, son of Ivan, a plaint as hereinafter detailed:

(1) Ivan Dovgochkhun, son of Nikifor, landowner, known to the whole world for his impious acts, which inspire universal repugnancy and violate the law in every way, did, on 7 July 1810, inflict a deadly insult, with direct bearing on my personal dignity and defamatory towards my rank and name. The aforementioned gentleman, besides being of loathsome appearance, is very quarrelsome by nature and nearly everything he says is blasphemous or insulting.

Here the secretary stopped to blow his nose again. The judge folded his arms admiringly and muttered to himself: 'What a lively pen! Good Lord, how that man can write!'

Ivan Ivanovich asked the secretary to carry on, and Taras Tikhonovich continued:

The said gentleman, Ivan Dovgochkhun, son of Nikifor, when I approached him with friendly intentions, did call me publicly by a most insulting and defamatory epithet, namely, a *goose*, whereas it is

133

known to all and sundry in the whole Mirgorod district that I was never christened after that disgusting animal, and I have no intention of being christened after it in the future. Evidence of my noble origin can be found in the baptismal register in the Church of the Three Bishops, in which is inscribed my date of birth and where my baptism is likewise recorded. Anyone with any pretension to learning will be aware that a goose is a bird, and not a human being; this fact must be familiar even to someone who has never attended a seminary. But the aforesaid malicious gentleman, being aware of all these facts, insulted me by using the aforementioned word with the sole intention of bringing the most terrible slander on my name and rank.

(2) This same indecent and gross gentleman did attempt to damage my property, inherited by me from my father, Ivan Pererepenko, clergyman and son of Onisyev, of blessed memory, in that, in flagrant violation of the law he erected a goose shed directly in front of my porch, with the sole intent of rubbing in the insult; for this afore-mentioned shed up to that time had stood in a very convenient position and was quite strong into the bargain. But the vile motive of the aforementioned gentleman consisted in this alone: viz.: to make me a direct witness of indecent actions, for it is known to everyone that no man goes into a shed – and least of all a goose shed – for reasons that can be mentioned in polite society. In carrying out this illegal act, the two front posts encroached on my land, handed down to me by my father when he was still alive, Ivan Pererepenko, son of Onisyev, of blessed memory, starting from the granary and extending in a straight line to the place where the women wash their pots.

(3) The gentleman described above, whose name inspires nothing but disgust, cherishes in his soul a desire to set fire to me in my own home. Indubitable evidence of this intention is substantiated by the following: firstly, the above-mentioned malicious gentleman has acquired the habit of leaving his house quite often, which never was the case formerly, on account of his laziness and revolting corpulence; secondly, in the servants' quarters, adjoining the fence, which encloses the land inherited from my father of blessed memory, Ivan Perere-penko, son of Onisyev, a light can be seen burning for an extraordinarily long time every day, which is irrefutable evidence, since hithertofore, as a result of his hateful niggardliness, not only the tallow candle, but even the oil lamp has always been extinguished during the day. And

therefore I request that the same gentleman, Ivan Dovgochkhun, son of Ivan, obviously guilty of arson, of insulting my name and family, of rapacious arrogation of my property and, worst of all, of appending the vulgar and offensive name of *goose* to my surname, be called to account by the court for full recompense, costs, and damages, that the criminal be put in irons and locked up in the town prison, and that judgement may be brought to bear on this my plaint without delay. Written and compiled by Ivan Pererepenko, son of Ivan, gentleman and landowner of Mirgorod.

When the plaint had been read out the judge went over to Ivan Ivanovich, grabbed hold of one of his buttons and spoke to him as follows:

'What are you thinking of, Ivan Ivanovich? Fear the Lord! Throw this plaint away, get rid of it! Send it to the devil! Shake hands with Ivan Nikiforovich, make it up with him, then go and buy some Santurinsky or Nikopolsky liqueur, or just make some punch, and invite me over! We'll all have a drink and forget the whole thing!'

'No, Demyan Demyanovich. It's not as easy as that!' Ivan Ivanovich said with that certain tone of authority that so became him. 'This is not something that can be cleared up by any mutual settlement. Good-bye. And good-bye to you gentlemen,' he continued, still with the same authority in his voice. Turning towards the clerks he said: 'I trust that the appropriate action will be taken.' And he walked out, leaving everyone in the courthouse utterly stupefied.

The judge sat down without a word. His secretary took a pinch of snuff, and the other clerks upset some broken pieces of bottle that served as inkwells. Even the judge, in a fit of absentmindedness, smeared a puddle of ink all over the table with his finger.

'And what do you think of that, Dorofei Trofimovich?' said the judge, turning to the clerk of the court after a short silence.

'I'd rather not say,' said the clerk.

'The things that happen nowadays,' the judge added. He had not had time to finish his sentence when the front door creaked and half of Ivan Nikiforovich made its appearance in the courtroom, leaving the hind portion outside in the vestibule. Ivan Nikiforovich's arrival was so unexpected that the judge gave a loud shriek. The secretary stopped reading. One of the clerks, clad in something made of frieze resembling a dress-coat, stuck his pen between his lips; another swallowed a fly. Even a soldier invalided out of the army who acted as messenger and warder as well – who up to this time had been standing by the door scratching himself through his dirty shirt with stripes on the arms – gaped and trod on someone's foot.

'To what do we owe this pleasure? How are you, Ivan Nikiforovich?'

But Ivan Nikiforovich was more dead than alive, as he had got stuck in the door and could not move forwards or backwards. It was a sheer waste of time the judge calling out into the vestibule for someone to shove Ivan Nikiforovich forwards into the courtroom. Only one old woman was there, with a petition, and although she pushed hard with her bony hands, she could not budge him. Then a thick-lipped clerk with broad shoulders, a fat nose, eyes that could not focus straight from drink, and with a jacket that was coming away at the elbows, went up to the front half of Ivan Nikiforovich, crossed his hands for him as though he were a child, and winked at the old soldier, who used his knee as a lever against Ivan Nikiforovich's belly; in spite of his pathetic groaning, he was squeezed out into the vestibule. Then the bolts were drawn back and the other half of the door opened. This combined effort made the clerk and the soldier breathe hard and as a result the whole court room was filled with such a strong smell it seemed to be momentarily transformed into a tavern.

'I hope I haven't hurt you, Ivan Nikiforovich. I'll ask my mother to send you a hot infusion to rub your back and stomach down with. That'll take the pain away.'

But Ivan Nikiforovich slumped down on a chair and all he was able to articulate was a continual stream of 'oh's.' Finally he said in a voice faint with exhaustion, 'Would you like some?' He took his snuff-box out of his pocket and added, 'Help yourself, please.'

'I'm very glad to see you,' the judge replied. 'But I still can't imagine why you have taken the trouble to come here and honour us with such an unexpected visit.'

'I've a plaint,' Ivan Nikiforovich burbled faintly.

'A plaint? What sort of plaint?'

'A summons . . .' At this point he completely ran out of breath and there was a long pause. 'Yes, a summons against that scoundrel . . . Ivan Ivanovich Pererepenko.'

'Good God! And you were such friends! How can you want to take proceedings against such a kind-hearted man?'

'He's the devil in disguise!' Ivan Nikiforovich snapped.

The judge crossed himself.

'Here's the plaint if you care to read it.'

'I suppose you'd better read it out then, Taras Tikhonovich,' the judge said, turning angrily to the secretary. At this point his nose took a sniff at his upper lip, something which normally only happened when he felt very pleased. To see his nose do just what it liked made the judge angrier still. He pulled out his handkerchief and wiped all the snuff off his upper lip to punish his nose for its audacity.

After he had gone through his usual nose-blowing performance before reading out documents the secretary began as follows:

Ivan Dovgochkhun, son of Nikifor, a gentleman residing in the Mirgorod district, presents his plaint in connection with the following:

(1) Through hateful malice and obvious ill-will, Ivan Pererepenko, son of Ivan, who calls himself a gentleman, has been inflicting on me every conceivable kind of harm, perpetrating damage and other pernicious acts which fill me with terror. Yesterday evening, just like a robber and a common thief, armed with axes, saws, chisels, and

various locksmith's tools, he climbed into my courtyard and then into my own goose shed, which is situated in the said courtyard. With his own hands, and in the most offensive manner, he chopped it down. On my part I gave no cause whatsoever for such illegal and outrageous behaviour.

(2) This same gentleman Pererepenko has been making attempts on my life, and on the 7th ultimo, concealing his real purpose, in the most insidiously friendly way, called on me and begged me to let him have my rifle, which was in my room, and with characteristic stinginess, offered in exchange several worthless things: his brown sow and two sacks of oats. Anticipating his criminal intentions, I tried in every way to put him off. But that same swindler and rogue, Ivan Pererepenko, son of Ivan, swore at me like a peasant and ever since has nurtured undying hatred towards me. Moreover, the said raging madman and confirmed criminal Ivan Pererepenko, son of Ivan, is of very low birth: everyone knows that his sister was a prostitute and followed a regiment of chasseurs which was stationed in Mirgorod five years ago. And she entered her husband in the register as a serf. His father and mother were also lawless people and incredible drunkards. The above-mentioned robber Pererepenko, in his bestial and venial behaviour, surpasses all his family and under the guise of piety does the most scandalous things. He does not fast, for on the eve of St Philip's Day this same heretic bought a sheep and the following day ordered his mistress to kill it, trying to justify himself by alleging that he needed tallow fat straight away for the lamps and candles. In the light of the foregoing I request that this landed gentleman, a declared robber, church thief, scoundrel, already found guilty of larceny and burglary, be clapped in irons and locked up in the town jail or government prison, and, under police escort, stripped of his rank and gentleman's status, before being given a thorough flogging and banished to forced labour in Siberia. And that he be ordered to pay costs and damages, and that judgement be carried out forthwith.

To this plaint Ivan Dovgochkhun, son of Nikifor, gentleman of the Mirgorod district, appends his signature below.

As soon as the secretary had finished, Ivan Nikiforovich grabbed his hat, bowed and made for the door.

'Where are you off to, Ivan Nikiforovich?' the judge

shouted. 'Please wait a minute! Stay for some tea. Oryshko, what are you standing there for, winking at the clerks, you stupid girl? Bring us some tea!'

But Ivan Nikiforovich, who was frightened at being so far from home territory, had already managed to squeeze through the door, saying as he left:

'Don't worry. It's really been a pleasure . . .' and with that he slammed the door after him, leaving everyone absolutely stupefied.

There was nothing that could be done.

Both plaints were filed and, just when events looked as if they might take quite an interesting turn, a totally unexpected incident made things even more interesting. As the judge was leaving the court with his clerk and secretary, and the other clerks were stuffing chickens, eggs, crusts, pies, biscuits and other oddments left behind by plaintiffs into a sack – at that very moment in rushed the brown sow and, to the amazement of the whole assembly, ignoring the pies and crusts, made straight for Ivan Nikiforovich's plaint, which was lying at the end of the table with some pages hanging down. Seizing the document, the brown porker ran off so quickly that not one of the clerks could catch it, despite the inkwells and rulers they flung after it.

This extraordinary event led to the most terrible confusion as no copy of the plaint had been made. The judge, his secretary and his clerk had a long debate about this unheard-of incident. Finally they decided to report it to the mayor, since the matter was really the concern of the police. Report no. 389 was dispatched that very same day, producing a rather curious sequel, as the reader will see in the next chapter.

5: In which is described the conference between two important personages of Mirgorod

As soon as Ivan Ivanovich had seen to things in the house and had gone out on to his veranda to have his customary rest, to his indescribable amazement he saw something red at the gate. This was the red cuff of the town provost's uniform, which, like the collar, was kept highly polished and resembled varnished leather along the edges. Ivan Ivanovich thought to himself: 'I'm rather pleased Pyotr Fyodorovich has come to talk it over,' but was surprised to see that the provost was walking extremely quickly and waving his arms – which was very unusual for him. He had eight buttons on his uniform, for the ninth had been torn off during a procession at the consecration of some church two years before, and the village police had not recovered it, although the mayor always used to ask if the button had been found when he read the daily reports handed in by the police officers. The way these eight buttons were set out was reminiscent of the way peasant women sow beans: one on the right, one on the left. He had been shot in the left foot during the last campaign and this made him limp and stick his leg out so far to one side that it almost cancelled out all the efforts of the other. The faster the mayor tried to make his 'walking machine' work, the less progress he made. Consequently, while he was struggling towards the veranda, Ivan Ivanovich had plenty of time to hazard a guess why the mayor was waving his arms so vigorously. The more he thought about it, the more importance he attached to this visit, especially as the mayor was carrying a new sword.

'Good morning, Pyotr Fyodorovich,' cried Ivan Ivanovich who, as we have already mentioned, was very inquisitive. He could hardly suppress his impatience as the mayor stormed the flight of steps up to the balcony, not looking up once and grumbling at his leg which he could not swing up the step at one go.

'Good day to my fine friend and benefactor, Ivan Ivanovich,' answered the mayor.

'Please sit down. I can see you're tired out, what with that crippled leg of yours . . .'

'My leg!' cried the mayor, giving him the kind of look a giant might give a pigmy, or a pedant a dancing-master. Then he stretched his leg out and stamped on the floor. This boldness cost him dearly, for his whole body lurched forwards and his nose struck the railings. However, this wise guardian of law and order tried to make out nothing had happened by immediately regaining his balance and feeling in his pocket for his snuff-box. 'I can tell you, my dear friend and benefactor Ivan Ivanovich, that never in all my born days have I ever made such an expedition. I mean that in all seriousness. Take the 1807 campaign . . . Ah, I could tell you how I once crawled under a fence to see a pretty little German girl.' At this the mayor winked and produced a diabolically roguish smile.

'Where have you been today?' asked Ivan Ivanovich, wishing to cut the mayor short and find out the reason for his visit as soon as possible. He was dying to ask what the mayor had to tell him, but his fine awareness of the ways of the world made him realize that such an approach would be indiscreet. And so Ivan Ivanovich had to hold himself in check and wait until the mayor spoke. All this time his heart pounded away with unusual force.

'Let me tell you,' the mayor answered. 'But first, I must inform you that it's very nice weather we're having . . .'

Ivan Ivanovich nearly died when he heard these last words.

The mayor continued, 'I've come to see you on a very important matter.' Here his face and bearing took on that same careworn appearance as when he was climbing up the steps.

Ivan Ivanovich breathed again, trembled feverishly, and came straight to the point as usual: 'Important matter? Why important?'

'Allow me to explain: may I inform you first of all, my dear friend and benefactor, Ivan Ivanovich, that you . . . from my point of view . . . I . . . let me explain, I've nothing to do with it, but that's what the law of the country demands. You have violated the rules of law and order . . . !'

'What's that? I don't understand at all.'

'Please, Ivan Ivanovich! What do you mean, you don't understand! An animal owned by you has stolen a very important government document and you can still say you don't understand!'

'What animal?'

'If I may say so, your own brown sow!'

'How am *I* to blame? Why did the court porter leave the door open?'

'But Ivan Ivanovich, the animal belongs to you, therefore you are guilty.'

'Thanks very much for putting me on the same level as a pig!'

'But I didn't say that, Ivan Ivanovich! Never! Just examine your own conscience: you must know that according to government law, unclean animals are prohibited from roaming around the town – and especially the main streets. You must agree that it's illegal.'

'God knows what you're talking about! So it's a great tragedy that a pig ran loose in the street!'

'Let me inform you, Ivan Ivanovich, that it's completely against the law. What are we going to do? The authorities say we must obey the law. I'm not denying that at times even chickens and geese run around the streets, even on the main square – just think of it! But only last year I issued an order for pigs and goats to be banned from the public squares. And I had that order read out in front of all the people.'

'No, Pyotr Fyodorovich, it's quite plain you're doing your level best to insult me in every possible way.'

'You can't mean that, my dear friend and benefactor. Just cast your memory back a little: last year I never said one word to you when you had a roof built two whole feet higher than is allowed. On the contrary, I pretended not to notice. My dearest friend, please believe that even at this stage, so to speak . . . but I have my duty to do, and I'm required to keep a close watch on public cleanliness. Just imagine if suddenly, in one of the main streets . . .'

'To hell with your main streets! All the women go there to dump any old rubbish they like.'

'Allow me to inform you, Ivan Ivanovich, that *you* are insulting me now! True, that does happen sometimes, but as a rule they dump their rubbish by fences, sheds or storehouses. But for a pregnant sow to go into the main street, or on to the square, is so . . .'

'Is so . . . what, Pyotr Fyodorovich? Surely a sow is one of God's creatures.'

'Agreed! Everyone knows you are a learned man, deeply versed in science, among other subjects. I never studied science myself, of course. I only learned to write longhand in the thirtieth year of my life. As you know, I came up through the ranks.'

'Hm,' Ivan Ivanovich muttered.

'Yes,' continued the mayor. 'In 1801 I was serving in the 42nd regiment of chasseurs, as a lieutenant in the fourth company. The company was commanded by a Captain Yeremeyev.' At this the mayor plunged his fingers into a snuff-box which Ivan Ivanovich held open, stirring up the snuff.

Ivan Ivanovich answered: 'Hm!'

'But it's my duty to observe the laws of the government. Did you know, Ivan Ivanovich, that it's a capital offence to steal an official document from a courtroom?'

'I'm well aware of that, and can tell you a thing or two in that respect. But stealing documents only applies to people: a pig is an animal, one of God's creatures!'

'That may be, but the law states: "those guilty of theft . . ." Listen carefully: *guilty*! No species is mentioned, or sex or rank, therefore an animal can be judged guilty. You can say what you like, but before sentence is passed the animal must be committed to the charge of the police as a common criminal.'

'No, Pyotr Fyodorovich!' exclaimed Ivan Ivanovich, 'You can't do that!'

'Say what you like, but I must carry out what the law demands.'

'Are you threatening me? Why don't you get that one-armed soldier of yours to go and arrest the sow? I'll tell one of my women to chase him off with a poker. Then he'll get his other arm broken.'

'I don't want to argue with you. Since you don't feel inclined to give the sow up to the police, then do what you like with it: kill it for Christmas and make some gammon, or eat it as it is. All I ask – in case you decide to make some sausages – is to send me a couple, you know, those that Gapka makes so well, with blood and fat. My Agrafena Trofimovna is very fond of them.'

'I'll send you a couple if you like.'

'I'd be very grateful, my dear friend and benefactor. And now allow me to say just one more thing: I have been instructed by the judge, as well as all our friends, to try and bring about a reconciliation between yourself and Ivan Nikiforovich.'

'What, with that ignoramus? With that boor? Never, never!'

Ivan Ivanovich was in a very determined mood.

'As you wish,' the mayor replied, regaling both his nostrils with snuff. 'I won't offer any more advice then, but just allow me to say, since you are on bad terms with him now, if you make it up . . .'

But Ivan Ivanovich started talking about quail shooting, which he usually did when he wanted to change the subject.

And so the mayor had no option but to go home, having achieved nothing.

6: From which the reader can easily discover its contents

IN spite of all the judge's efforts to hush the matter up, by the next day all Mirgorod knew that Ivan Ivanovich's sow had stolen Ivan Nikiforovich's plaint: the judge in a moment of absentmindedness forgot himself and was the first to let the cat out of the bag.

When Ivan Nikiforovich heard about it, all he did was reply: 'Was it the *brown* one by any chance?'

But Agafya Fedosyevena, who was there at the time, started nagging Ivan Nikiforovich again. 'What's the matter with you? Everyone will laugh and think you're a complete idiot if you don't do something. And you won't be fit to call yourself a gentleman any more. You'll be lower than the women who sell those sweetmeats you're so fond of!'

And the terrible nagger managed to persuade him to take action. Somewhere she found a swarthy middle-aged man with spots all over his face, who wore a dark-blue frock-coat patched at the elbows – a regular government pen-pusher! He blacked his boots with tar, wore three pens behind his ear, and instead of an inkwell had a glass phial tied to his buttonhole by a piece of bootlace. He could eat as many as nine pies at once, keeping a tenth in his pocket, and was a master at filling one sheet of chancery notepaper with so much libel that no one could read it through at one go without coughing and sneezing in between. This pitiful semblance of a man messed around in the files, scribbled away for all he was worth, and finally concocted the following statement:*

To the District Judge of Mirgorod from the gentleman Ivan Dovgochkhun, son of Nikifor:

Pursuant to my aforesaid plaint presented to me, Ivan Dovgochkhun, son of Nikifor, conjointly with that of the aforesaid Ivan Pererepenko, son of Ivan, concerning which the Mirgorod District Judge has demonstrated his own illegal connivance. And that the said taking the law into its own hands on the part of the sow being furtively concealed and becoming known through third disinterested parties. Inasmuchas

*Besides being a parody of the legal officialese of the day, this passage is *intentionally* meaningless in parts, being concocted by a half-witted clerk with a smattering of legal knowledge. (Trans.)

the aforesaid criminal admission and illegal connivance being maliciously contrived must forthwith be judged in a court of law; inasmuchas the aforesaid pig is a stupid animal and thus all the more capable of documentary embezzlement. From which it is obviously evident that this oft-mentioned pig was incited by our opponent, to wit, Ivan Pererepenko, son of Ivan, calling himself gentleman, and already convicted of robbery, attempted murder, and sacrilege. But the aforesaid Mirgorod Court, with its characteristic partiality gave its authority clandestinely. For without such authority the aforesaid pig could never have gained entry to the courthouse to carry off the documents. Inasmuchas the Mirgorod Court is well supplied with staff, we need only adduce as evidence one invalided soldier who is always to be found in the vestibule and who, despite having only one eye and a rather crippled arm, has abilities proportionate to the task of chasing off the said pig and clubbing it with a large cudgel. From which is patently evident the illegal connivance of the aforesaid Mirgorod Court and the indisputable mutual distribution of the profits accruing therefrom as a result of Jew-like double dealing. The same aforesaid abovementioned robber has thus incriminated himself in larceny. Therefore I, Ivan, a gentleman son of Nikifor, Dovgoch-khun, bring proper and fitting notification to the ears of the Court that: if the aforementioned plaint concerning the abovementioned brown sow (or the gentleman Pererepenko in league with it) is not investigated and decided in my favour and advantage, then, I, Ivan, gentleman, son of Nikifor, Dovgochkhun, will take the plaint to the High Court about the illegal connivance according to the fit and proper formal transference of the matter. Signed, Ivan, gentleman, son of Nikifor, Dovgochkhun, of the Mirgorod District Court.

This plaint had the desired effect. Like all good people, the judge was a timid man. He consulted his secretary. But the secretary produced a throaty 'Hm' and displayed that indifferent and diabolically equivocal expression assumed only by Satan himself when he sees his victim rushing to throw himself at his feet. Only one course of action remained open to him: to reconcile the two friends. But how was he to set about this, when all efforts up to now had been futile? However, he decided to have one more try. But Ivan Ivanovich told him straight out he would not hear of it and, what was more, became very angry, while Ivan Nikiforovich answered by turning his back on him and not saying a word.

Subsequently the case proceeded with that abnormal rapidity our courts normally pride themselves on. Documents were dated, entered, numbered, sewn together, recorded – all in one day, and the case was filed away in a cupboard where it just lay and lay and lay, one, two, three years. During that time many girls found themselves husbands; a new street was laid out in Mirgorod; one of the judge's double teeth fell out, together with two eye-teeth; more children than ever ran around Ivan Ivanovich's yard – God knows where they came from. Ivan Nikiforovich, to insult Ivan Ivanovich, built a new goose-shed, slightly further back than the other one, and completely blocked himself off from him, so that these worthy gentlemen hardly ever set eyes on each other. And the papers continued to lie in the cupboard, which became mottled with ink-spots. Meanwhile an event of the greatest importance for Mirgorod took place. The mayor gave a reception. Where can I find brush and palette to portray the varied gathering at that magnificent banquet? Take your watch, open it up and see what's going on inside. You won't deny that it's absolute chaos. Now try and imagine about the same number of wheels – if not more – all standing in the mayor's courtyard. What carriages and waggons there were there! One was wide behind and narrow in the front, another narrow behind and wide in the front, a third a carriage and waggon combined, and a fourth neither carriage nor waggon. One looked like a huge haystack or a fat merchant's wife, another resembled a dishevelled Jew or a skeleton not quite freed from the skin. Another, if you viewed it from the side, looked just like a pipe with a long stem, while yet another looked like nothing on earth, suggesting some strange, shapeless, absolutely fantastic object.

In the middle of all this chaos of wheels and coach boxes one could glimpse what appeared to be a carriage with a lattice shuttered window – just like in a house. The drivers, in grey Cossack overcoats, short Ukrainian coats, sheepskin hats and caps of varying sizes, drove the unharnessed horses through the courtyard. What a reception the mayor gave! If you will allow me, I will just run through the guests.

There were: Taras Tarasovich, Evpl Akinfovich, Evtikhy Evtikhiyevich, Ivan Ivanovich (another one), Savva Gravrilovich, our own Ivan Ivanovich, Elevfery Elevferiyevich, Makar Nazaryevich, Foma Grigoryevich . . . that's enough for now, I've no strength left, my hand's tired with all this writing. And the ladies! Dark- and fair-complexioned, short and tall, some of them fat, like Ivan Nikiforovich, and others so thin, you could easily picture them hiding in the scabbard of the mayor's sword. And the hats and dresses! Red, yellow, coffee-coloured, green, blue, new, turned, re-cut; and the shawls, ribbons, and handbags! Farewell, my poor eyes! You will never see properly again after such a sight. And the long table they laid out! What a noise they made with all their chatter – a mill, with all its stones, wheels, pinions and cogs would be silent in comparison. I can't tell you exactly what they talked about, but the conversation must have been about a whole host of pleasant and useful subjects, such as the weather, dogs, wheat, nightcaps, colts. Finally Ivan Ivanovich – not ours, but another Ivan Ivanovich with one eye – said:

'Strange, but my right eye (this Ivan Ivanovich always talked sarcastically about himself) does not see Ivan Nikiforovich Dovgochkhun.'

'He didn't want to come,' the mayor replied.

'Why not?'

'Good God, it's already two years since they had their quarrel – I mean Ivan Ivanovich and Ivan Nikiforovich; if one of them knows where the other is, you can't drag him there for all the tea in China!'

'What are you talking about!' The one-eyed Ivan Ivanovich

looked up and folded his arms. 'If people with *good* eyes can't get on together, how am I supposed to live on good terms with everyone, seeing I've only one eye?'

This produced a loud guffaw. Everyone loved the one-eyed Ivan Ivanovich for his witticisms which suited the modern taste extremely well.

A tall thin man in a felt coat, with a plaster on his nose, who until then had been sitting in the corner with a face that remained absolutely motionless, even when a fly flew up his nose, left his seat and joined the crowd surrounding the one-eyed Ivan Ivanovich.

'Listen,' the one-eyed Ivan Ivanovich said when he saw a fair crowd had gathered round him. 'Instead of staring at my bad eye, why don't we try and get our two friends to make it up! Ivan Ivanovich is having a chat with the women and girls right now – let's send for Ivan Nikiforovich on the quiet, and then bring them together.'

This proposal met with universal approval and they decided to send someone round to Ivan Nikiforovich's and try and persuade him to come to the mayor's house for dinner without fail. But the important question – whom to entrust with this difficult mission – foxed everyone.

For a long time they argued as to who was best versed in the methods of diplomacy. Finally they decided unanimously to entrust Anton Prokofyevich Golopuz with the job.

But first we must acquaint the reader with this outstanding personage. In every sense of the word, Anton Prokofyevich was a highly virtuous man: if one of Mirgorod's worthy citizens happened to give him a scarf or some item of underwear he would *thank* him.

He would also thank someone for giving him a gentle rap on the nose. If anyone were to ask him, 'Why are you wearing a brown frock-coat with blue sleeves?' he would usually reply: 'But *yours* isn't like mine. You wait, when it begins to wear out, it will be the same colour all over!' And it was just as he said: the sun turned the blue cloth of the sleeves brown, so it was a perfect match for the rest of the coat. But the strange thing was that Anton Prokofyevich had the habit of wearing woollens in the summer and nankeen in the winter. Anton Prokofyevich does not have a house of his own now. He did have one once, on the outskirts, but he sold it, and with the proceeds bought a team of three horses and a small carriage, in which he rode around visiting the local landowners. But as he had a lot of trouble with the horses, and needed money for oats, Anton Prokofyevich exchanged them for a violin and a housemaid, plus a twenty-five-rouble note. Then he sold the violin, and exchanged the girl for a gold and morocco tobacco pouch. And now he has a pouch like no one else. Because of this little luxury he cannot go riding around the villages any more, but has to stay in the town and spend the night at different houses, especially where the owners take delight in flipping him on the nose. Anton Prokofyevich is quite a gourmet, and plays a good hand at cards.

He has always loved taking orders and immediately set off with his hat and cane. However, as he walked along, he began to wonder how he could best persuade Ivan Nikiforovich to come to the reception. But the stubbornness displayed by that otherwise very worthy gentleman rendered his task almost impossible.

And how on earth could he make him come, when it was an effort for him just to get out of bed? But supposing he did get up – how could *anyone* expect him to come to a place where he knew without any shadow of doubt he would find his mortal enemy?

The more Anton Prokofyevich reflected, the more obstacles he found. It was a stifling day, the sun beat down, and the sweat just poured off him. Although he did get rapped on the nose from time to time, Anton Prokofyevich was quite a cunning man in many ways. He was not so good when it came to bargaining, however. He knew when to pretend to be stupid and could sometimes extricate himself from certain tricky situations where a clever person would be all at sea.

While his inventive mind was cooking up some way of persuading Ivan Nikiforovich to come (he had already set off bravely on his mission) he was rather put out by something he was not expecting at all. At this stage there would be no harm in mentioning that, among other things, Anton Prokofyevich had such a peculiar pair of trousers that when he wore them dogs always bit him in the calves of the leg. Unfortunately he was wearing this pair of trousers that day, and he had not progressed very far in his deep reflections before his ears were deafened by a terrifying barking all round him. Anton Prokofyevich yelled so loud – no one could yell as loud as him – that not only one of the peasant women he knew came rushing out with the boy in the vast coat, but all the brats from Ivan Ivanovich's yard as well. Although the dogs managed to get their teeth into one leg only, this had a shattering effect on his ardour and he approached the front steps very warily.

7: And the Last

'Ah, good morning! Why are you tormenting the dogs?' said Ivan Nikiforovich – everyone made a joke of it when they talked to somebody like Anton Prokofyevich.

'Tormenting the dogs? I wish they'd all drop dead!' answered Anton Prokofyevich.

'You're lying!'

'On my life I'm not! The point is that Pyotr Fyodorovich wants you to come to dinner.'

'Hm.'

'You know, I really can't tell you how badly he wants you to come. "Why", he said, "does Ivan Nikiforovich avoid me like the plague? He never drops in for a chat, or a little natter . . ."'

Here Ivan Nikiforovich started stroking his chin.

'Something else he said: "If Ivan Nikiforovich doesn't come now, I shan't know what to make of it, and I'll begin to think he has evil designs on me. Do me a favour, and *make* him come!" Well, what are we sitting here for? Let's go! There's a wonderful crowd there.'

Ivan Nikiforovich began scrutinizing a cock which stood on the porch crowing for all it was worth.

The conscientious messenger continued: 'If you could only see the sturgeon and fresh caviar Pyotr Fyodorovich's been sent!'

At this point Ivan Nikiforovich turned around and began to listen attentively, which encouraged the messenger.

'Let's not waste any more time! Foma Grigoryevich is there as well!' Then, seeing Ivan Nikiforovich was still lying in exactly the same position, he added: 'Well, are we going or not?'

'I don't want to.'

This '*I don't want to*' startled Anton Prokofyevich. He had already begun to think he had won that worthy man over by his persuasive arguments. But all he had achieved was a determined 'I don't want to'.

'But why not?' he said, speaking in a tone of annoyance, which was extremely rare for him, even when people put burning paper on his head – a trick which the judge and the mayor were very fond of playing on him.

Ivan Nikiforovich took a pinch of snuff.

'Just as you like, Ivan Nikiforovich, but I don't see what's holding you back.'

'What do I want to go for?' he muttered at length. 'That cut-throat will be there!' (He was in the habit of calling Ivan Ivanovich by this name.)

'I swear to God he won't be there! May I be struck down by lightning if he is!' answered Anton Prokofyevich, who was prepared to swear ten oaths within a single hour. 'Let's go, Ivan Nikiforovich!'

'I can see that you're lying, Anton Prokofyevich: he *is* there!'

'By all that's holy, I swear he's not. May I never leave this house if he's there! And just think, why should I tell you lies? I'd rather my legs and arms withered and fell off! What, you still don't believe me? May I be struck dead before your very eyes! Let my father and mother, and me as well, never reach heaven! You still don't believe me?'

With these assurances Ivan Nikiforovich's mind was set completely at rest and he ordered his valet (the boy in the enormous coat) to fetch his baggy trousers and nankeen cossack coat.

I imagine it is quite unnecessary to describe how Ivan Nikiforovich put on his trousers, or how his valet tied his cravat and finally pulled on his cossack coat, which burst under the left sleeve. Suffice it to say he remained cool and collected throughout the operation and ignored Anton Prokofyevich's offer of swapping something for his Turkish tobacco pouch.

Meanwhile the whole assembly impatiently awaited the critical moment when Ivan Nikiforovich would turn up and the reconciliation would take place between the two worthy gentlemen – something everyone hoped for. Many of them felt certain that Ivan Nikiforovich would not come. The mayor even wanted to bet the one-eyed Ivan Ivanovich that he would not turn up, but withdrew when this Ivan Ivanovich offered to stake his own bad eye against the mayor's crippled leg, a suggestion which infuriated the mayor, but made everyone else laugh to themselves. No one had sat down to eat yet, although it was long past two – by which time everyone in Mirgorod has usually eaten, even on special occasions like this.

As soon as Anton Prokofyevich appeared at the door everyone crowded round. All inquiries met with a categorical 'He's not coming.' He had hardly said this, and a hail of reproaches, abuse and perhaps even little raps was already descending on his head for failing in his mission, when suddenly the door opened and in came Ivan Nikiforovich. If Satan himself or a ghost had appeared, they would not have created such a sensation as Ivan Nikiforovich's unexpected arrival. But Anton Prokofyevich nearly split his sides laughing and was tickled pink at having made everyone look so silly.

However Ivan Nikiforovich had managed it, no one could really believe he had dressed himself up to look like a gentleman in such a short time. Ivan Ivanovich was not there at that moment, having gone outside. When they had recovered from their amazement, everyone inquired about Ivan Nikiforovich's health and said they were pleased to see he had put on weight. Ivan Nikiforovich kissed them all and said: 'I'm very grateful.'

Meanwhile the smell of borshch drifted across the room and agreeably titillated the nostrils of the hungry guests. They all piled into the dining-room. Quiet ladies and talkative, fat ladies and thin, all surged forward together, and the long table suddenly shone with every conceivable colour. I shall not attempt to describe all the courses. I will remain silent about the dumplings and sour cream, and the giblets served with the borshch, and the turkey with plums and raisins, or the dish that closely resembled a pair of old boots soaked in kvass*, and the sauce, the swan song of the old-fashioned chef – a sauce which was served enveloped in brandy flames, which the ladies found very amusing as well as frightening. I shall not describe these dishes because I prefer eating them to expatiating about them. Ivan Ivanovich was delighted with the fish dressed with horseradish. He picked the finest bones out, laid them on the plate, and then happened to glance across the table. God in heaven, he could not believe his eyes! Ivan Nikiforovich was sitting opposite!

At that very moment Ivan Nikiforovich happened to glance up ... No, I can't go on! ... Bring me a different pen to describe the scene, mine has gone sluggish and dead; its nib is

*kvass – national peasant drink made from rye bread and malt. (Trans.)

154

too fragile. Their faces registered mutual amazement and seemed to turn to stone. Each saw a familiar face opposite him, a face he could quite easily have approached, without even thinking about it, offering some snuff with the words: 'Please take some' or 'I shall esteem it a favour.' But now those faces looked terrifying, omens of some disaster to come. The sweat just poured off Ivan Ivanovich and Ivan Nikiforovich.

All the guests looked on numbly and did not take their eyes off the former friends for a single second.

The ladies, who up to this point had been engaged in a very interesting conversation on the preparation of capons, suddenly cut their discussion short. Everything went quiet. Only a great painter could have done the scene justice.

Finally Ivan Ivanovich pulled out his handkerchief and started blowing his nose, while Ivan Nikiforovich looked around until his eyes came to rest on the open door. The chief of police noticed this at once and ordered the door to be shut. Then the friends started eating without giving each other so much as a glance.

As soon as dinner was over, the two former friends leapt from their seats and started looking for their hats with the intention of making their escape.

Then the mayor winked and Ivan Ivanovich – the one with the bad eye – stationed himself behind Ivan Nikiforovich, while the mayor took up a similar position behind Ivan Ivanovich, and both tried to pull them backwards towards each other, not intending to release them until they shook hands. The one-eyed Ivan Ivanovich – although by a slightly devious route – managed to push Ivan Nikiforovich towards the spot where Ivan Ivanovich was standing; but the mayor steered too much to one side, on account of his wayward leg, which on this occasion disobeyed all orders and, as if out of spite, kicked out in the opposite direction, possibly under the influence of the startling variety of drinks that had been served at dinner, making Ivan Ivanovich fall over a lady in a red dress who, out of curiosity, had pushed her way into the middle of the room. This was a very bad omen.

To put things right the judge took the mayor's place, and after sweeping all the snuff from his upper lip with his nose pushed Ivan Ivanovich in the opposite direction.

This is the usual way they try to make things up in Mirgorod, and it is rather like playing a ball game. As soon as the judge had given Ivan Ivanovich a shove, the one-eyed Ivan Ivanovich strained every muscle and pushed as hard as he could against Ivan Nikiforovich, from whom perspiration was streaming like rainwater from a roof. Although the two friends put up a stiff resistance, they were at last pushed together with the help of strong reinforcements from the other guests.

Then they were closely hemmed in and not released until they had agreed to shake hands.

'Come now, Ivan Nikiforovich and Ivan Ivanovich! Look in your hearts and tell us what the quarrel's about. You must admit it's about nothing at all. Don't you feel ashamed before everyone, and before God?'

'I don't know,' Ivan Nikiforovich said, breathless from exhaustion (you could see that he was on the point of being reconciled). 'I really don't know what I did to annoy Ivan Ivanovich. Why did he chop my goose-shed down and try to ruin me?'

'I'm not to blame for any evil plots against you,' Ivan Ivanovich said without looking at Ivan Nikiforovich. 'I swear before God and before all you good people that I never harmed my enemy. Why did he have to drag my name in the mud and slander my rank and family?'

'And what *harm* have I done you, Ivan Ivanovich?' said Ivan Nikiforovich.

Just one minute more, and the quarrel would have been patched up. Ivan Nikiforovich was already feeling about for his snuff-box, to offer it with his usual 'Please take some, do.'

'If it isn't harm, then what is it,' answered Ivan Ivanovich, looking down, 'when you called me by such an indecent word that I really can't repeat it in polite society?'

'As one friend to another, Ivan Ivanovich,' (at this point Ivan Nikiforovich touched one of Ivan Ivanovich's buttons, a sure sign that he was ready to make it up) 'God knows what I said to cause offence, because I only called you a *goose* . . .'

Ivan Nikiforovich saw immediately that he had committed a terrible blunder in saying this word, but it was too late: he had said it!

All was lost . . .

Ivan Ivanovich had already lost his temper once before when this word was said without anybody else there to hear it, and had flown into such a rage (God spare us from such a spectacle again!) that our dear readers can judge for themselves the effect when the fateful word was pronounced before a large social gathering, with many ladies present, and in whose company Ivan Ivanovich was particularly careful about his language. Things would not have been so bad if Ivan Nikiforovich had said *bird* instead of *goose* – the matter could have still been put right. But all was lost now.

What a look he gave Ivan Nikiforovich! If that look had had any physical power behind it, it would have literally pulverized Ivan Nikiforovich. The guests realized this and tried to separate them. And that same gentleman, a model of humility, who would not let a beggar woman go past without asking if she needed anything, rushed out in the most terrible rage. So violent are the storms aroused by human passions!

For a whole month nothing was heard of Ivan Ivanovich. He shut himself up in his house. The ancestral chest was opened and the old silver roubles that belonged to his grandfather were taken out. These silver roubles passed into the inkstained hands of legal scribes. The case went to the High Court. And only when Ivan Ivanovich received the glad tidings that the case would be decided the following day did he take a look at the outside world and decide to come out of the house. But, alas, from that time onwards the court announced each day that the case was going to be decided tomorrow, and this went on for ten years!

Five years ago I happened to be passing through Mirgorod. I had picked a bad time. It was autumn, and the weather was miserable – damp and misty, with mud everywhere. A kind of unnatural green substance – produced by continual, tiresome rain – covered the fields with a watery pattern.

At that time I was very sensitive to the weather – when it was miserable, so was I. In spite of this, my heart started beating violently when I approached Mirgorod. The memories the place holds for me! It was twelve years since I had visited the town, where two men who were quite inseparable had lived in a friendship which was touching to see. How many important people had died since then! Judge Demyan Demyanovich had passed away, and the one-eyed Ivan Ivanovich had breathed his last. I went into the main street; everywhere there were poles with bundles of straw tied on the top. Some large-scale alterations were in progress. A few huts had been pulled down. The remains of wattle fences and hedges stuck out depressingly.

It was a high holiday. I ordered the covered carriage to stop at the church, and went in very quietly, so that no one would notice. But I need not have worried. The church was almost deserted, and there was hardly anyone there at all. Evidently the mud had frightened away even the most pious. The candles looked strangely unpleasant in that gloomy, rather sickly light. The dark porch had a melancholy look, and the oblong windows with their circular panes were streaming with tears of rain. I went into the porch and approached a venerable-looking old man with grey hair: 'Do you know if Ivan Nikiforovich is still alive?'

At that moment the lamp in front of the icon flared up and the light shone straight into the old man's face. You can imagine how astonished I was to see those familiar features again. It was Ivan Nikiforovich himself. But how he had changed!

'Are you keeping well, Ivan Nikiforovich? Goodness, how you've aged!'

'Yes, I have indeed. I've been to Poltava today.'

'What's that! You went to Poltava on a day like this?'

'What else can I do? There's a lawsuit pending . . .'

At this I could not help sighing. Ivan Nikiforovich noticed and said: 'Don't worry. I've had news from a reliable source that the case will be decided next week, and in my favour.'

I shrugged my shoulders and went off to see what I could find out about Ivan Ivanovich.

'Ivan Ivanovich is here,' someone said. 'Over there, in the choir.'

Then I saw a thin figure. Was that really Ivan Ivanovich? His face was covered with wrinkles and his hair had turned white. But he was still wearing the same short fur coat. After we had greeted each other, Ivan Ivanovich turned to me with that cheerful smile which suited his funnel-shaped face so well and said: 'Have you heard the good news?'

'What news?' I asked.

'My case will be decided tomorrow without fail. The High Court said it's absolutely certain.'

I heaved an even deeper sigh, hurriedly made my farewell, as I had some very important business, and I climbed on to my covered cart. Some gaunt-looking horses, known as couriers in Mirgorod, made an unpleasant squelching as they trod in the grey mass of mud. The rain poured down on a Jew who was sitting on the horse box with a mat over him.

The dampness soaked right through me. The wretched turnpike with its sentry box, with an old soldier sitting there repairing his rifle, slowly passed by. Those fields again, with black, ploughed patches showing among the green; drenched crows and jackdaws; monotonous rain, and a tearful sky without one ray of sunlight shining through the clouds . . . It's a depressing world, gentlemen!

Ivan Fyodorovich Shponka and His Aunt

BEHIND this story there is another one. We first heard it from Stepan Ivanovich Kurochka who had just travelled up from Gadyach. Now, one thing you must know is that I have an absolutely shocking memory. You can talk to me until you are blue in the face, but everything goes in one ear and out the other. It's like trying to fill a sieve with water. As I am only too aware of this weakness of mine I asked our visitor to write the story down for me specially in an exercise book. He was always kind to me, God grant him good health, and he took the book and wrote everything out. I put it on the small table, which I think you know: it stands in the corner near the door. Oh dear, I quite forgot, you have never even been here! My old housekeeper, who has been with me for thirty years now, never learned to read and write and there's no point in trying to disguise the fact. Once I noticed she liked baking pies on paper. Dear reader, she bakes absolutely wonderful pies, better than you'll eat anywhere. So I had a look underneath them and what do I see but some writing. It was as if I'd known deep down already – I went up to the table and there was half of the exercise book gone! She had torn the pages out for her pie paper! What can you do? You can't quarrel at our time of life!

Last year I had to pass through Gadyach. So before I even got near the place I tied a knot so I shouldn't forget to ask Stepan Ivanovich about it. I'd assured myself that as soon as I sneezed in the town, this would make me remember to call on him. But it was all no use: I travelled through the town, sneezed, blew my nose in my handkerchief, and still forgot to call. At least, I didn't remember until I was about four or five miles from the town gates. So there remained nothing else to do but print the story without an ending. However, if anyone really wants to know what happened in the end, all he has to do is go to Gadyach and ask Stepan Ivanovich. He will take great pleasure in telling you the story, although he'll insist on starting right from the beginning. He doesn't live very far from the stone church. You'll find a little lane there, and as soon as you turn into it, it's the second or third gate along. Better still, when you see a large pole with a quail on it and a fat woman wearing a green skirt (there's no harm in my saying that Stefan leads the life of a bachelor) then you'll know it's his place. However, you could also try the market, where you can catch him every morning before nine choosing fish and green vegetables and having a chat with Father Antip or a Jewish merchant. You'll recognize him at once, for no one else has the same printed linen trousers or yellow cotton coat. And there's something else you can recognize him by: he always walks about waving his arms. The late lamented local assessor Denis Petrovich always used to say when he spotted him coming some way off: 'Look! Look! Look at our windmill over there!'

Ivan Fyodorovich Shponka

IT is already four years since Ivan Fyodorovich Shponka retired and settled down on his farm at Vytrebenky. When he was still a little boy he went to the local school at Gadyach and I must say he was exceedingly diligent and well-behaved. The Russian grammar teacher, Nikifor Timofeyevich Deyeprichastiye used to say that if all his other boys applied themselves like Shponka there would be no need for that maplewood ruler of his. He was fed up with caning idlers and mischief-makers, as he himself was the first to admit.

His exercise book was always immaculate, with a ruled margin and not a mark anywhere. He would always sit very quietly, his arms folded, his eyes riveted on his teacher. He never hung bits of paper on the back of the boy in front, never made carvings in the desks, and never played at shoving other boys off the benches just before the teacher came in. If anyone needed a knife for sharpening a pen, then he would go straight away to Ivan Fyodorovich, knowing he was bound to have one. Ivan Fyodorovich (at that time he was simply called Vanusha) would take it out of its small leather sheath which he kept tied to the buttonhole of his greyish coat, and all he asked was that the sharp edge was not to be used for pens, insisting there was a blunt side for that. Before long his industriousness caught the attention of the Latin teacher, the sound of whose cough in the corridor was enough to terrify the whole class even before his woollen overcoat and pockmarked face made their appearance at the classroom door.

This frightening teacher, who always had two bundles of birch twigs lying on his chair, with half the boys kneeling in subjection around it, made Ivan Fyodorovich class monitor, although there were many far better qualified for the job.

Here we must not forget to mention one incident which was destined to have a lasting influence on the whole of his life. One of the boys under his command brought a buttered pancake wrapped in paper into the class, hoping this would induce his monitor to pass his work with a *scit*, whereas in fact he had not prepared his lesson at all.

Now, although Ivan Fyodorovich was usually quite conscientious, on this occasion he was very hungry and could not resist the temptation. He took the pancake, propped his book in front of him and began eating. He was so absorbed that he did not even notice the deathly silence that suddenly fell on the class. And it was only when he looked up in horror that he realized what was happening. By then that terrible hand sticking out of its woollen jacket had seized him by the ear and dragged him out into the middle of the room. 'Give me that pancake! Give it to me, you miserable wretch!' roared the terrible teacher, who snatched the pancake and flung it out of the window, with a strong warning to the boys running around the playground not to dare pick it up. After this he gave Ivan Fyodorovich a severe and very painful caning on the hands. According to his reasoning the hands alone were guilty, since they had taken the pancake and no other part of the body should therefore be punished. Anyway, from that time onwards his timidity – the first thing that struck you about him and which was quite bad enough already – grew even more pronounced. Perhaps this incident was the reason why he never showed any desire to enter government service, since experience had taught him it is not always possible to conceal one's crimes.

He was very nearly fifteen when he entered class two, where instead of the abridged catechism and four rules of arithmetic he grappled with more complex matters, such as the duties of man and fractions. But when he saw that the further one advances, the more pitfalls lie in the way, and when he heard that his father had taken leave of this world, he stayed on another two years and then, with his mother's consent, entered the P— Infantry Regiment. The latter was quite different from most normal infantry regiments, and, despite being stationed in little country villages most of the time, lived it up in such style that even most *cavalry* regiments could not compete with it. Most of the officers drank strong spirits made from frozen liquor and even the Hussars could teach them nothing about pulling Jews around by their ringlets. A few of them even danced the mazurka, and the colonel never missed the opportunity of mentioning this when he was at social gatherings. Patting himself on the belly after each word, he used to say: 'Many of my officers dance the mazurka; a great many, my dear sir, oh, *ever* so many.'

To give the reader another example of the P— Regiment's high cultural level, we should add that two of the officers were so passionately fond of playing banker that they gambled away their uniforms, peak caps, greatcoats, sword knots, even their underclothes, something you would hardly ever come across even among *cavalry* regiments. Rubbing shoulders with such friends, however, did not make Ivan Fyodorovich any less shy. Since he never drank strong spirits, preferring a glass of vodka before dinner or supper, and since he did not dance the mazurka and did not play cards, quite naturally he was always left to his own devices. And so, when the others went gallivanting around on hired horses visiting small landowners, he stayed in his room doing the sort of thing you might expect of someone so meek and mild: sometimes he would polish his buttons; sometimes he would read a fortune-telling book, sometimes he would set up mousetraps in the corners of his room; sometimes he would just throw his uniform off and lie on his bed. But then, there was no one in the whole regiment so punctilious as Ivan Fyodorovich, and he drilled his platoon so well that the Company Commander always set him up as a shining example to the rest. Therefore, in a very short time, only eleven years after becoming an ensign, he was promoted second lieutenant.

During this period he learned from his aunt that his mother had passed away. This aunt (his mother's sister) he knew only because when he was a boy she used to bring by hand or send him (even as far as Gadyach) dried pears and very tasty honey cakes she made herself. She was on bad terms with his mother and so he had not seen her since his childhood. Now this aunt, being very kind-hearted, took over the management of his small estate, and duly informed him of this. Since Ivan Fyodorovich was quite sure his aunt was a very capable person, he carried on his military duties. Anyone else in his place would have gone around boasting about his important promotion. But pride was quite foreign to his nature, and after he became a second lieutenant he was just the same Ivan Fyodorovich as he had been when he was a mere ensign. When he had spent another four years in the army after this wonderful event in his life, and was getting ready to travel with the regiment from Mogilev* to Russia proper, he received the following letter:

My dear nephew Ivan Fyodorovich,

I'm sending you some clothes: five pairs of cotton socks and four fine linen shirts. There's something I'd like to mention. As you've already reached quite an important rank, I think by now you should realize you're quite old enough to think of managing the estate, and there's no point in your staying on in the army. I'm getting on in years and I can't look after everything. There's a lot I want to talk to you about *personally*. So do come home, Vanyusha.

Looking forward to seeing you,
Your loving Auntie,
Vasilisa Tsupchevska.

P.S. The turnips in the kitchen garden are simply wonderful this year, more like potatoes than turnips.

Ivan Fyodorovich answered a week later:

Dear Auntie Vasilisa,

Many thanks for the clothes. In fact, my socks are so worn out my batman has darned them four times. As a result they've become very tight.

About my staying on in the army, I quite agree with what you say and three day ago I resigned my commission. As soon as I get my papers I'll try and hire a cart.

I've had no luck at all with that seed-wheat and Siberian corn you asked me to get. There's none in the whole Mogilev province. They feed the pigs here mainly on brewer's mash mixed with a little stale beer.

Your affectionate and ever-loving nephew,
Ivan Shponka.

Finally Ivan Fyodorovich was retired with the rank of full lieutenant. He found a Jew to take him from Mogilev to Gadyach for forty roubles, and climbed into the covered cart just at that time of year when the trees were still sparsely clothed with young leaves, when the whole earth shone bright with fresh greenery and all the fields were fragrant with spring.

*Mogilev was in the Ukraine or 'Little Russia', a region with a large Jewish population. (Trans.)

2. On the Road

NOTHING very eventful happened during the journey, which took just over two weeks. Ivan Fyodorovich might have arrived sooner, but the orthodox old Jew had to celebrate the Sabbath by sticking his horse-cloth over his head and praying all day long. However, as I have mentioned before, Ivan Fyodorovich was not the kind of person to let himself get bored waiting.

While the Jew was at his devotions he unlocked his trunk, took out his linen, checked it over to see if it was properly laundered and folded, carefully picked the fluff off his new uniform, which was made without epaulettes, and then put everything back as neatly as he could. He was not very fond of reading; but if he chanced to look at a fortune-telling book it was because everything in it was familiar and he had already read it several times before, just as someone living in a town goes off to the club every day, not to hear anything new, but to meet those friends whom he is used to chatting to from time immemorial. In the same way a clerk in the civil service reads the address book with great enjoyment several times a day, not from any *ulterior* motives, but because he simply loves reading a list of names in print. 'Ah, there's Ivan Gavrilovich So-and-so!' he says in a toneless voice. 'Ah, there's my name. Hm!' And then he reads it all over again, making exactly the same comments.

After two weeks' journey Ivan Fyodorovich reached a small village about eighty miles from Gadyach. This was on a Friday. The sun had set some time before he drove up to the inn with his Jew and his covered waggon. This inn was no different from any others you find in small villages. Usually no effort is spared to regale the traveller with hay and oats, just as if he were a post-horse. But if he wants a proper meal, like any *respectable* person, then he is obliged to conserve his appetite for another time.

Ivan Fyodorovich knew all about this and had equipped himself beforehand with two bundles of dough rings and a sausage. He asked for a glass of vodka, which *no* inn is short of, and sat down to supper at an oak table which was firmly riveted to the clay floor.

While he was eating his supper he suddenly heard a small carriage draw up. The gates creaked open, but it was some time before the carriage actually drove into the yard. He could hear a loud voice quarrelling with the old woman who owned the inn.

'All right, I'll stay the night, but if I'm bitten by a single bug then I'll smash your face in, you old bag! And I won't pay for the hay either!'

A minute later the door opened and there entered, or should I say there *squeezed* in, a fat man in a green jacket. His head was immovably fixed on a short neck, which was made to look even thicker by his double chin. Apparently he belonged to the class of people who have never let *little* things get them down and whose whole life has been plain sailing.

'Pleased to meet you, my dear fellow,' he said when he saw Ivan Fyodorovich.

Ivan Fyodorovich bowed and did not reply.

'And may I ask whom I have the honour of addressing?' the fat stranger asked.

This cross-examination made Ivan Fyodorovich involuntarily stand to attention, which he normally did when the colonel was speaking to him.

'Retired lieutenant Ivan Fyodorovich Shponka,' he answered.

'And may I ask where you're going?'

'To my estate, Vytrebenky.'

'Vytrebenky!' his formidable inquisitor exclaimed. 'Allow me, my dear sir!' he said, going up to him and waving his arms about as if someone were trying to hold him back, or as if he were struggling through a crowd. He came up to Ivan

Fyodorovich and embraced him, kissing him first on the right cheek, then on the left, then again on the right. Ivan Fyodorovich did the same and found this kissing very enjoyable, as the stranger's large cheeks made soft cushions for his lips to plant themselves on.

'Please, my dear sir, allow me to introduce myself,' continued the fat man. 'I've an estate in the Gadyach district as well, and I'm your neighbour. I live at Khortishche, not more than four miles from Vytrebenky. My name's Grigory Grigoryevich Storchenko. We must, we really *must* get together, my dear sir. And I won't have anything to do with you if you don't come and visit me at Khortishche. But now I'm in rather a hurry . . . What's that?' he asked a boy who came in wearing a cossack-style short overcoat with patched elbows, a startled look on his face, and who began laying out bundles and boxes on the table.

'What's going on, eh?' Grigory Grigoryevich's voice grew more and more threatening. 'Did I tell you to put these here? Well, did I, you little devil? Didn't I tell you to warm the chicken up first? Get out!' he shouted, stamping his foot. 'Wait a minute, you with the ugly mug. Where's the hamper with the bottles?'

'Ivan Fyodorovich,' he added, pouring some liqueur into a glass, 'do have some of my medicine!'

'No, really, I've had a drink already,' Ivan Fyodorovich said hesitantly.

'I won't hear of it, my dear chap,' the landowner said, raising his voice. 'I just won't hear of it! I'm not leaving this place until you join me . . .'

When he saw it was impossible to refuse, Ivan Fyodorovich drank a glass, which he did not find exactly unpleasant.

'This is *some* bird, my dear sir,' the fat Grigory Grigoryevich continued, carving it inside a wooden box. 'I must inform you that my cook Yavdokha sometimes has a drop too much and as a result everything gets overdone. Hey, step lively,' he said to the boy in the overcoat, who at that moment was carrying in a feather bed and some pillows. 'Lay my bed out in the middle of the room. And mind you put plenty of hay under the pillow. And pull some hemp from the women's distaff to stop my ears up with when I go to bed. I must tell you, my dear sir, that I've had the habit of stuffing up my ears when I'm in bed ever since that damned night when I was staying in some Russian* inn and a cockroach crawled into my left ear. Those blasted Russians, as I found out later, drink their cabbage soup with cockroaches in it. I can't describe what happened. There was such a tickling in my ear I felt like banging my head against a brick wall. A simple old woman helped me out in the end. And how do you think she did it? Just by whispering. What do you think about our doctors, my dear chap? All those devils do is make complete fools of us. Old peasant women know twenty times as much as all your doctors.'

'You're perfectly right,' said Ivan Fyodorovich. 'In fact...' At this point he stopped, as if he could not think of the right word. Here it won't hurt to mention that Ivan Fyodorovich was not really what you might call eloquent. Perhaps this was because of his shyness, or perhaps because he was always looking for better words.

'Give it a good shake now,' Grigory Grigoryevich said to his boy. 'The hay's so rotten here you'll get nasty twigs sticking out if you don't watch it. Allow me to wish you a very good night, my dear sir! We shan't see each other tomorrow, as I'm leaving before dawn. Your Jew will be praying all day, as it's a Saturday, so there's no point in your getting up early. Don't forget now, I won't have anything to do with you if you don't come and visit me at Khortishche.'

Here Grigory Grigoryevich's valet pulled his jacket and socks off for him and put a dressing-gown over him. Grigory Grigoryevich slumped on to his bed, which made it look as if

*Note: the action is taking place in the Ukraine, not in Russia proper. (Trans.)

one great feather mattress were lying on top of another.

'Aha, look alive there! Where have you gone, you devil? Straighten the blankets out. Move yourself, and put more hay under my head. You've watered the horses, haven't you? More hay. Under *this* side. Now straighten that blanket out properly. That's it, some more. Ah!'

Grigory Grigoryevich sighed twice more and then filled the whole room with terrifying nasal whistles; now and again he snored so loud that the old woman dozing on the bench by the stove would wake up, peer round the room, and, relieved at finding nothing wrong, would drop off again.

When Ivan Fyodorovich woke up next day the fat landowner had already gone. This was the only event of note throughout the whole journey. Three days after this he was approaching his little farm. He felt his heart pounding when he saw the windmill waving its arms about, and as the Jew drove his nag higher up the hill he could see rows of willows spreading beneath him. The pond glinted through them, lending its freshness to everything. At one time he used to go swimming in that same pond, or wade up to his neck after crayfish with the other boys from the village. The cart reached the top and Ivan Fyodorovich at once caught sight of that same old-fashioned little house thatched with rush, those same apple and cherry trees he used to climb up when no one was around. The moment the cart entered the yard, dogs of every description came running from all directions: chestnut-coloured, black, grey, spotted. Some ran barking around the horse's hooves, others went round the back when they smelled the axle greased with fat. Another stood by the kitchen with its paw over a bone and howled for all it was worth. Another could be heard barking some way off as it ran backwards and forwards, wagging its tail as if to say: 'Look, everyone, what a fine young dog I am!' The village boys came running in their dirty shirts to see what was going on. A sow taking a stroll around the yard with its sixteen piglets lifted up its snout with an inquiring look and gave a louder grunt than usual. Around the yard were scattered sheaves of wheat, millet and barley all drying in the sun. On the roof different kinds of wild grass such as chicory and swine-herb had been left to dry as well.

Ivan Fyodorovich was so engrossed with all this that he only came to his senses when the spotted dog bit the Jew on the thigh as he was climbing down from the cart. The household servants, comprising one cook, one old woman and two girls in woollen shifts all came running up. After shouting 'Oh, our young master's back!' they announced that Auntie was planting Indian corn in the kitchen garden with the help of Palashka and Omelko the coachman, who performed the duties of kitchen gardener as well. But Auntie had spotted the covered cart when it was still some way off and now arrived on the scene. Ivan Fyodorovich was astonished when she almost lifted him right off his feet and could hardly believe this was the same Auntie who had written complaining she felt poorly and was getting too old to cope.

3. AUNTIE

AT that time Aunt Vasilisa Kashporovna was about fifty. She had never married and used to say she valued a spinster's life more than anything else. Still, if my memory serves me right, no one had ever courted her. This was because she made everyone feel shy and no one could pluck up the courage to propose. Her suitors used to say, 'Vasilisa Kashporovna has a *very strong* character.' And they were right, since Vasilisa Kashporovna always wore the trousers. She could transform the drunken miller (who was not fit for anything) into a perfect treasure, just by pulling him by his curly tuft of hair every day with her own very manly hands. She looked like a giant and in fact had the proportions and strength of one. It seemed as if Nature had committed some unforgivable blunder in decreeing she should wear a dark-brown cloak with flounces on weekdays and a red cashmere shawl on Easter Sundays and her name-day, when a dragoon's moustache and high jackboots would have suited her much better. And the way she spent her time was a perfect reflection of what she wore: she went boating, wielding the oars even more skilfully than the fishermen themselves; she went shooting wild game, and was for ever standing over the reapers at work; she could tell you exactly how many melons there were in the kitchen garden, and she made anybody who crossed her pastures in their waggon pay a toll of five kopecks; she climbed trees and shook the plums down; she beat her lazy vassals with that awesome hand of hers – and that same terrible hand would offer a glass of vodka to those who earned it. Almost simultaneously she would tell everyone off, dye yarn, cook honey, make jam, bustle around the whole day, and still manage to get everything done. As a result, Ivan Fyodorovich's little estate (according to the last census there were eighteen serfs) was flourishing in the true meaning of the word. What's more, Auntie was extremely fond of her nephew and carefully put away every kopeck she could save for him.

After his arrival Ivan Fyodorovich's life was completely transformed. It seemed as if Nature had created him specially to run that farm with its eighteen serfs. Even Auntie remarked that he would make a good farmer, but all the same did not let him have a say in *everything* to do with running the estate. Although Ivan Fyodorovich was not far short of forty she used to say: 'He's only a *young boy*, so how can you expect him to know everything?'

However, he was always to be found in the fields with the reapers and haymakers, something which brought inestimable pleasure to his gentle ears. The sweep of more than ten shining scythes in unison; the noise of grass falling in orderly rows; the reapers breaking into song – gay songs for welcoming guests, sad ones for farewells; calm, fresh evenings – and what evenings! How free and pure the air is then! How everything springs to life! The steppe flames with red, then blue, simply burning with the colours of the flowers. Quails, bustards, gulls, grasshoppers, thousands of insects – all of them whistling, buzzing and chirping away, then breaking into one melodious chorus! Nothing is silent for one moment and the sun sets and hides below the horizon. Ah, how fresh and good it is! Here and there fires are lit in the fields, copper cauldrons are set up and the reapers gather round them. Steam rises from the dumplings. Dark turns to grey . . . It is hard to say how Ivan Fyodorovich felt at these times. He would stand next to the reapers and forget to help himself to dumplings, a dish he was very fond of, standing motionless and following the flight of a gull disappearing into the heavens, or counting the sheaves of harvested wheat strung out over the fields like beads.

It was not long before Ivan Fyodorovich acquired the reputation of a first-class farmer. However, Auntie never admitted to being satisfied, although she never missed the opportunity of singing her nephew's praises. One day, towards the end of the harvesting, at the end of July to be exact, Vasilisa Kashporovna took Ivan Fyodorovich by the hand and with a mysterious look said she wanted to have a chat with him about something that had been on her mind for a long time.

'My dear Ivan Fyodorovich,' she began, 'you know very well there are eighteen serfs on the farm. However, that's only according to the last census, and by now there are probably twenty-four. But that's not what I want to talk to you about. You know that little forest with the broad meadow on the other side? Not far short of sixty acres. And the grass is so lush, you can earn yourself more than a hundred roubles a year – especially if the cavalry happens to be stationed at Gadyach.'

'Why, of course I know, Auntie. The grass is very good there.'

'I know that without *you* telling me. But did you know that all that land is yours? Why are you goggling like that? Listen, Ivan Fyodorovich? You remember Stefan Kuzmich? Are you listening? You were so small then, you couldn't even pronounce his name. I remember I came just before Advent and took you in my arms and you nearly ruined my dress. Luckily I managed to plump you on your nurse Matryona. You were so dirty then! But all that's neither here nor there. All the land on the other side of our farm, and the village of Khortishche too, belonged to Stefan Kuzmich. Before you were born he used to ride over to see your mother. Of course, only when your father was out. But I'm not reproaching her for it, God rest her soul, even though she always treated me very unfairly. But that's another story. Anyway, Stefan Kuzmich, by deed of title, left you that estate I was talking to you about. But your late mother (strictly between ourselves), behaved very strangely at times. The Devil himself (God forgive me for using such a disgusting word) would have a job understanding her. And where she put that title deed, God only knows. I think that old bachelor Grigory Grigoryevich Storchenko has it. That pot-bellied old devil managed to grab the whole estate, and I'd stake my life on it that he's got that deed hidden away somewhere.'

'May I ask, dear Auntie, if that's the same Storchenko I met at the inn?'

Here Ivan Fyodorovich told her about the meeting.

'Who knows?' she answered after a moment's reflection. 'Perhaps he's not a swindler after all. True, it's only six months since he came to live near us and you can't get to know anyone in such a short time. The old woman, his mother, is a very sensible woman and is a dab hand at pickling cucumbers. And her maids make wonderful carpets. But if as you say he was very friendly, then go and see him. Perhaps the old rake's conscience will prick him and he'll give up what doesn't belong to him. You could have taken the small carriage, only those damned brats have pulled all the nails out of the back. You must tell Omelko to fasten the leather covering down much better in future.'

'Why do I need the carriage, Auntie? I'll take the old waggon, the one you use when you go shooting wildfowl.'

And with that the conversation ended.

4. THE DINNER

IT was around dinner time when Ivan Fyodorovich entered the village of Khortishche and he felt certain misgivings as he approached the landowner's house. It was a long building, not thatched with reeds like other local landowners' houses, but with a wooden roof. The two barns in the yard had wooden roofs as well. The gates were made of oak. Ivan Fyodorovich felt like a dandy who arrives at a ball and sees that everyone is dressed more smartly than he is. Out of respect he left the old cart by one of the barns and walked the rest of the way to the front door.

'Ah, Ivan Fyodorovich,' fat Grigory Grigoryevich shouted as he crossed the yard, wearing a coat, but without any tie, waistcoat or braces. However, even these clothes were evidently too heavy and thick for someone of his size, for the sweat just poured off him. 'Didn't you say you'd come and visit me *as soon as* you'd seen your Auntie again?' After these words Ivan Fyodorovich's lips were welcomed by the familiar cheek cushions again.

'I've been very busy on the farm. I've only dropped in for a few minutes, because there's something I want . . .'

'Just for a few minutes? We can't allow that. Hey, step lively,' he shouted and the same boy in the cossack-style overcoat came running from the kitchen. 'Tell Kasyan to shut the gates, and mind he does it properly! And unharness this gentleman's horses immediately. Please come in. It's so hot out here my shirt's soaked through.'

Ivan Fyodorovich went inside. He made up his mind not to waste any time, to try and overcome his shyness and get right down to business.

'My Auntie has the honour, so she said . . . to inform you that the late Stefan Kuzmich's deed of title . . .'

It is hard to imagine the expression these words produced on Grigory Grigoryevich's broad, expansive face.

'Good God! I can't hear a thing!' he answered. 'I must tell you that a cockroach once crawled into my left ear. Those blasted Russians have started breeding the things in their huts. No pen could describe the torments I went through. It just went on tickling and tickling. An old woman got rid of it very simply . . .'

'What I wanted to say,' said Ivan Fyodorovich, taking the liberty of interrupting Grigory Grigoryevich, who was clearly trying to change the subject, 'what I wanted to say was that this deed of title is mentioned in the late Stefan Kuzmich's will, and in connection with this . . .'

'I know what your aunt's been saying. A complete lie, I tell you! My uncle made no such deed of title. However, *something* like that's mentioned in the will, but where is it? No one's ever produced it. I'm telling you this, as I sincerely want to help you. I swear to God it's all a lie!'

Ivan Fyodorovich said nothing, and reflected that perhaps Auntie had really imagined everything.

'Ah, here comes Mother with my sisters,' said Grigory Grigoryevich. 'That means dinner's ready. Come on!' And with that he caught hold of Ivan Fyodorovich by the hand and pulled him into the next room, where there was a table laden with vodka and savouries. At this moment an old, shortish woman came in, a real coffee-pot in a nightcap, accompanied by two girls, one fair, the other dark. Ivan Fyodorovich, like the gentleman he was, first went up to kiss the old lady's hand, then kissed the hands of the two young ladies.

'Mother, I want to introduce a neighbour of ours, Ivan Fyodorovich Shponka!' said Grigory Grigoryevich.

The old lady stared at Ivan Fyodorovich, or at least, so it appeared. All she wanted to do, it seemed, was to ask Ivan

Fyodorovich how much salt he used for pickling cucumbers during the winter.

'Did you have some vodka before you came?' she asked.

'Mother, you can't have had a proper nap,' said Grigory Grigoryevich. '*Who* asks a guest if he's had anything to drink *before* he arrives. You should offer him some, whether *we've* had any or not. Ivan Fyodorovich, some centaury flavoured or Trokhimov vodka? Which do you prefer? Ivan Ivanovich, why are you standing there?' Grigory Grigoryevich added, turning round. And Ivan Fyodorovich saw the gentleman of this name go up to the vodka in his long-tailed frock-coat with its enormous stand-up collar covering the whole of the back of his neck, which made his head look as though it were riding in a carriage.

Ivan Ivanovich went up to the vodka, wiped his hands, had a good look at his glass, poured some vodka out, lifted it up to the light, poured the whole glassful into his mouth, rinsed it round without swallowing it right away – and then gulped it down. After he had eaten some bread with some salted golden-brown mushrooms he went up to Ivan Fyodorovich.

'Do I have the pleasure of addressing Ivan Fyodorovich Shponka?'

'That's right, sir.'

'You've changed a lot since I saw you last. I remember when you were as tall as this,' continued Ivan Ivanovich, putting his hand about two feet from the floor. 'Your late father, God rest his soul, was a man of rare qualities. No one could grow melons like he did.' Then he continued, drawing Ivan Fyodorovich to one side: 'Those melons you get here – you can't call them melons, they're not even worth looking at! Believe me, my dear sir,' he added with a mysterious expression, opening his arms wide apart as if he were trying to embrace a thick tree, 'they were this size, I swear it!'

'Let's go in to dinner,' Grigory Grigoryevich said, and took Ivan Fyodorovich by the arm. Everyone went into the dining-room. Grigory Grigoryevich sat at his usual place at the end of the table. With his enormous napkin he looked like one of those heroes painted by barbers on their shop signs.

Ivan Fyodorovich sat blushing in his appointed place opposite the two girls. And Ivan Ivanovich did not let the chance slip of sitting next to him, terribly pleased that there was someone present to whom he could show off his knowledge.

'It's no good looking for the parson's nose, Ivan Fyodorovich,' the old lady said, turning to him. 'It's a hen turkey.' At this moment a waiter in a grey frock-coat with black patches all over it put a plate in front of him. 'Have some of the back.'

'Mother!' Grigory Grigoryevich said. 'Please don't interfere. You can rest assured our guest knows what he wants! Ivan Fyodorovich, have some wing . . . There . . . Why have you taken so little? Have some leg.' Then he turned to the waiter and said: 'Why are you standing there gaping with that plate? Ask him to take some. Down on your knees, you old devil. Now ask our guest: "Ivan Fyodorovich, please take some leg".'

The waiter went down on his knees and bellowed: 'Do take some leg, Ivan Fyodorovich.'

'Hm, do you call that a turkey?' Ivan Ivanovich said to his neighbour in a contemptuous, low voice. 'If you want real turkeys, you should see mine! I swear any one of them has more fat on it than ten of these. Believe me, it makes you feel quite sick to see them running round the yard, they're so fat!'

'You're lying, Ivan Ivanovich,' said Grigory Grigoryevich, who had overheard this little speech.

Ivan Ivanovich pretended he had not heard and carried on talking to his neighbour: 'I'm telling you that last year, when I sent them to Gadyach, I got fifty kopecks each. And I wouldn't take it.'

'And I say you're lying,' Grigory Grigoryevich said, in a louder voice this time, clearly enunciating each syllable. But

Ivan Ivanovich pretended this remark was not directed at him at all and continued, in a lower voice this time: 'Yes, I wouldn't take it. Not one farmer in Gadyach . . .'

'Ivan Ivanovich, you're nothing but an idiot!' shouted Grigory Grigoryevich. 'Ivan Fyodorovich knows more about these things than you and won't believe a word you're saying.'

Ivan Ivanovich was very hurt by this remark. He did not say any more and started devouring the turkey – even though it was not as fat as those which make you feel sick just to look at them.

The clatter of knives, spoons and plates took the place of conversation for a while; but the loudest noise of all was made by Grigory Grigoryevich sucking the marrow out of a sheep's bone.

After a short silence Ivan Ivanovich stuck his head out of its 'carriage' and asked Ivan Fyodorovich: 'Have you read Korobeinikov's *Journey to the Holy Land*?* It's a book to delight the heart and soul! They don't publish books like that nowadays. I'm only sorry I forgot to see what year it came out.'

When Ivan Fyodorovich heard the subject had changed to books he diligently applied himself to the sauce.

'My dear sir, I find it quite amazing that a simple commoner from the town should have visited all those places. More than two thousand miles! More than two thousand miles! Why, it's as if Our Lord Himself, by His divine grace, enabled him to visit Palestine and Jerusalem.'

Ivan Fyodorovich, who had heard a lot about Jerusalem from his orderly, remarked:

'You said he visited Jerusalem?'

'What did you say, Ivan Fyodorovich?' Grigory Grigoryevich asked from the other end of the table.

'I had occasion to remark that the earth contains many far-off places,' said Ivan Fyodorovich, deeply pleased with himself for producing such a long and difficult sentence.

*A work written in 1583, but not published until 200 years later. (Trans.)

'Don't believe him, Ivan Fyodorovich,' said Grigory Grigoryevich, who evidently hadn't heard properly, 'he does nothing but tell lies.'

Dinner was over. Grigory Grigoryevich went off to his room for his usual little nap, while the guests followed the old lady and the two girls into the drawing-room where that same table at which they had been drinking vodka before dinner had undergone a transformation and was now covered with dishes containing various kinds of jam and plates of melons and cherries.

Grigory Grigoryevich was conspicuous by his absence. The old lady became very talkative and, without being asked, revealed a great many secrets about making fruit jelly flans and drying pears. Even the girls opened their mouths. But the blonde, who seemed six years younger than her sister and who was actually about twenty-five, was not so talkative. Ivan Ivanovich was livelier and said more than anyone else. Convinced that no one would try to contradict or muddle him, he talked about growing cucumbers and sowing potatoes, about how sensible everyone was in the old days – how *could* you compare people at present? – and about how things were progressing and what wonderful inventions were being made. He was one of those people who take the greatest pleasure in sweetening their souls with conversation and will talk about anything and everything under the sun. If the conversation happened to be on a solemn or religious subject, then Ivan Ivanovich would sigh after each word and quietly nod. If the conversation turned to more domestic matters, he would stick his head out of its 'carriage' and make such faces you could tell from his expression alone how to make kvass* from pears, how enormous those melons were, and how fat those geese running around his yard.

Finally, when it was already evening, Ivan Fyodorovich

*kvass: a home-brewed drink, usually made from rye bread and malt. (Trans.)

managed to bid them farewell, but only after great difficulty. Despite his easy-going nature and pliancy, and although his hosts very nearly forced him to stay the night, he would not give in and succeeded in making his escape.

5. AUNTIE'S NEW PLAN

'WELL, did you get the deed out of the old devil?' This was the question Ivan Fyodorovich's aunt greeted him with on his return. She was so impatient that she had been waiting several hours on the front steps and in the end could not resist running out to the main gate.

'No, Auntie,' Ivan Fyodorovich said as he climbed down from the cart. 'Grigory Grigoryevich has no deed of title.'

'And you believed him! He's lying, damn him! If I ever meet him, I'll thrash him with my own hands. *I'll* strip that fat off him! Anyway, we'd better have a talk with our solicitors to see if we can take him to court over it. But that's neither here nor there. Did you have a good meal?'

'Yes, very good, Auntie.'

'Well, what did you have? I know the old girl's an excellent cook.'

'There were cheese fritters with sour cream, Auntie. And stuffed pigeons with sauce . . .'

'Did you have turkey and plums?' asked Auntie, who was an expert at preparing that very same dish.

'Yes, we had turkey as well. He's got two very pretty sisters, Grigory Grigoryevich, especially the blonde!'

'Ah,' said Auntie and stared at Ivan Fyodorovich, who blushed and looked down at the ground. A new thought suddenly flashed through her mind. 'Well then,' she asked in a brisk, inquisitive voice, 'what were her eyebrows like?'

Here we should mention that Auntie always thought a woman's eyebrows were the most important part of her looks.

'Her eyebrows, Auntie, were just like the ones you said you

had when you were young. And she's got little freckles all over her face.'

'Ah!' said Auntie, very pleased with this observation, although in fact he had not meant to pay her this compliment.

'What kind of dress was she wearing? Nowadays it's hard to find the high quality material my cloak's made of. But that's neither here nor there. What did you find to talk about?'

'Talk? Me, Auntie? Perhaps you're already getting ideas . . .'

'Well, what's so strange about that? It's all in the hands of the Good Lord. Perhaps you were destined from birth to get married.'

'I don't know how you can say that, Auntie. It only goes to show you don't know me at *all*.'

'Oh, I've really touched a soft spot there!' said Auntie. 'A little boy,' she thought, 'he knows nothing! I *must* bring them together, and at least let them get to know each other.'

Here Auntie left Ivan Fyodorovich and went into the kitchen. But from now on all she thought about was seeing her nephew married as soon as possible and herself looking after some little grandchildren. She imagined the preparations for the wedding, and everyone noticed she was fussing around much more than usual, with the result that things took a turn for the worse, instead of improving. Often, when she was making a pie (normally she would not trust the cook with this), her thoughts would wander. She would imagine a little grandson was standing by her asking for a piece. Absent-mindedly she would hand him one of the best pieces, but one of the house dogs, seeing its chance, would seize the tasty morsel and wake her from her daydreams with its loud munching: for this it was invariably beaten with a poker. She even neglected her favourite pastimes and did not go shooting so often; once she even shot a crow instead of a partridge, something she had never done before.

Four days later everyone saw the old carriage rumbling out

of its shed into the yard. Omelko, the coachman (he was night watchman and looked after the kitchen garden as well) had been hammering away from early morning, nailing on new leather, and chasing off the dogs when they tried to lick the grease off the wheels. I must inform my readers that this was the very same carriage that Adam travelled in. And if you meet anyone trying to pass his carriage off as Adam's, then you can be sure that it must be a complete fake, an absolute forgery if ever there was one. God alone knows how it ever survived the Flood. One can only conclude that there was a special shed for it in Noah's ark. It's a pity I haven't time to describe it in detail. Suffice it to say that Vasilisa Kashporovna was very satisfied with the way it was made and was forever expressing her deep regret that carriages in the old style had gone out of fashion. Its actual structure – it tilted slightly to one side so it was much higher on the right than the left – was very much to her liking, since it could accommodate a large person on one side and small ones on the other. It could take five small grandchildren and three people the same size as Auntie.

Towards the afternoon Omelko led three horses out of the stables – three horses not much younger than the carriage – and began harnessing them to the magnificent vehicle with a rope. Ivan Fyodorovich and his aunt – one from the left, the other from the right – climbed into the carriage and drove off. When the peasants they passed along the road saw such a sumptuous carriage (Auntie rarely used it) they respectfully stopped, took off their hats and bowed very low. Two hours later the carriage came to a halt (I need hardly say where) at the front door of Storchenko's house. Grigory Grigoryevich was not in. The old lady and the two girls met the visitors in the dining-room. Auntie swept up to them quite magnificently, gracefully put one leg forward and said in a loud voice:

'Very glad to offer you my respects, and to thank you personally for being so hospitable towards my nephew Ivan

Fyodorovich who speaks highly of the welcome you gave him. What marvellous buckwheat you grow! I saw it when I drove up to the village. Do you mind telling me how many sheaves per acre you get from it?'

Thereupon everyone started kissing each other. When they were all settled in the drawing-room the old lady began:

'I can't tell you anything about the buckwheat, that's Grigory Grigoryevich's concern. I haven't had anything to do with that for a long time now, because I'm too old and incapable! I remember in the old days that our buckwheat used to grow right up to one's waist. God knows what it's like now, though they do say it's even better.' Here the old lady sighed. Anyone present would have detected in this sigh an echo of the eighteenth century.

'I hear your maids make wonderful carpets,' Vasilisa Kashporovna said, touching the old lady's most sensitive chord. At these words she livened up and started babbling away about dyeing yarn and preparing thread. From carpets the conversation quickly changed to pickling cucumbers and drying pears.

'Well, would you like to have a look?' the old lady said, getting up.

Vasilisa Kashporovna and the girls stood up as well and they all went into the maids' room. However, Auntie signalled to Ivan Fyodorovich to stay where he was and whispered something to the old lady.

'Mashenka,' the old lady said, turning to the blonde sister. 'Stay and talk to our guest, so that he won't be bored.'

The blonde girl stayed behind and sat on the couch. Ivan Fyodorovich shifted about in his chair as though it was full of needles, blushing and looking down at the floor. But the young lady apparently did not notice this and sat quite coolly on the couch, carefully inspecting the windows and walls and watching the cat, which had taken fright and was running around under the chairs.

Ivan Fyodorovich plucked up a little courage and tried to say something. But all the words seemed to get lost on the way. Not a single thought came into his head. The silence lasted about a quarter of an hour. All this time the young lady just sat there.

Finally Ivan Fyodorovich made a great effort and said in a trembling voice:

'There's a lot of flies this summer, Miss.'

'Oh, thousands,' she answered. 'My little brother made a swatter out of one of Mama's old shoes; but the place is still full of them.'

The conversation came to an end once more. Ivan Fyodorovich could not think of anything to say at all.

Finally the old lady, Auntie, and the dark-haired sister returned. After chatting a little while longer Vasilisa Kashporovna took her leave, despite repeated invitations to stay the night. The old lady and the sisters came out on to the front steps with their guests to say good-bye, and for a long time stood there curtseying to Auntie and her nephew, who kept on looking back out of the departing carriage.

'Well, Ivan Fyodorovich, what did you talk about?' Auntie asked as they drove along.

'She's a very unpretentious, well-bred young lady, Marya Grigoryevna!'

'Listen, Ivan Fyodorovich, I want to have a serious talk with you. Good God, you're thirty-eight now. You have a good position. It's time to think about having children. You must get yourself a wife . . .'

'*What*, Auntie!' Ivan Fyodorovich cried out in horror. 'A wife! No, Auntie, please! You're making me blush! . . . I've never been married before, I just wouldn't know what to *do* with a wife!'

'You'll find out,' she said, smiling, 'you'll find out.' Then she said to herself: 'Whatever next? He's just like a child!' Then she continued aloud: 'Yes, Ivan Fyodorovich, you couldn't find a better wife than Marya Grigoryevna. And you're quite attracted to her, I know. I've had a chat with the old lady, and she'll be more than delighted to have you as her son-in-law. Of course, we still don't know what that old devil Grigory Grigoryevich will have to say. But let's not think about him. And if he doesn't give her a dowry, we can always take him to court . . .'

At this moment the carriage was approaching the yard and the ancient steeds livened up, sensing they were not far from their stable.

'Listen, Omelko, let the horses rest before they have a drink: they're hot from the journey.' She climbed down and said, 'Ivan Fyodorovich, I advise you to consider this very carefully. Right this minute I'm needed in the kitchen. I forgot to tell Solokha about dinner and that lazy bitch won't have thought of doing anything herself.'

But Ivan Fyodorovich stood there thunderstruck. True, Marya Grigoryevna was quite pretty; but to get *married*! The idea seemed so inconceivable, so far from his world, that he just could not think about it without a profound feeling of terror. Live with a *wife*! It was just unheard of! He would never be alone in his room any more, because there would always be *two* of them, together, everywhere! The sweat poured off his face the more engrossed he became in these thoughts. He went to bed earlier than usual, but, however hard he tried, he just could not drop off.

In the end long-awaited sleep, that universal comforter, descended on him. But what dreams he had! He had never known such chaotic nightmares before. First he dreamt that everything around him was making a terrific din and whirling round and he was running, running, without feeling the ground under his feet, until he could run no longer. Suddenly someone grabbed him by the ear. 'Ah, who's that?' 'It's me, your wife!' a voice shouted right into his ear. And he suddenly woke up. Then he had another dream, that he was already married, that everything in the house had become very strange and peculiar, and that there was a *double* instead of a single bed in his room. His wife was sitting on a chair. He was completely at a loss what to do, whether to go up to her or speak to her, and then he noticed that she had the face of a goose. He looked the other way, and saw another wife, and she had a goose's face as well. He looked again and there was a third wife; he looked around – still another. He panicked and ran into the garden, but it was hot out there. He took off his hat – and there was a wife sitting in it. Beads of sweat trickled down his face. He felt in his pocket for his handkerchief – and found a wife in it. He took some cotton wool out of his ear – there was a wife there too. Suddenly he started jumping around, and Auntie looked at him and said in a serious voice: 'Yes, you may well jump around, because you're a married man now.' He went over to her, but Auntie had turned into a belfry and someone was hauling him up by a rope to the top. 'Who's pulling me up?' he asked in a pathetic voice. 'It's me, your wife, and I'm hauling you up because you're a bell.' 'No, I'm not a bell, I'm Ivan Fyodorovich!' he shouted. 'No, you're a bell,' said a certain colonel of the P— infantry regiment who happened to be passing at the time. Then he had another dream, that his wife was not a person at all, but some kind of woollen material. He had gone into a shop in Mogilev. 'What kind of material would you like, sir?' asked the shopkeeper. 'Have some *wife*, it's the latest thing now! Lovely quality as well. Everyone's having coats made from it.' The shopkeeper made his measurements and cut the wife up. Ivan Fyodorovich took it under his arm and went off to a Jewish tailor, who said, 'No, that's *very poor* material. No one uses *that* kind of stuff for coats now . . .' Ivan Fyodorovich woke up terrified, with cold sweat pouring off him.

As soon as he got up he consulted his fortune-telling book, at the end of which some philanthropically-minded bookseller, out of rare kindness of heart and unprompted by any *mercenary* motives, had put in an abridged *Intrepretation of Dreams* as an appendix. But he could not find anything even remotely resembling such a mad dream.

Meanwhile Auntie had hatched a new plan which you will learn more about in the next chapter.

More about Penguins

Penguinews, which appears every month, contains details of all the new books issued by Penguins as they are published. From time to time it is supplemented by *Penguins in Print*, which is a complete list of all available books published by Penguins. (There are well over four thousand of these.)

A specimen copy of *Penguinews* will be sent to you free on request. For a year's issues (including the complete lists) please send 30p if you live in the United Kingdom, or 60p if you live elsewhere. Just write to Dept EP, Penguin Books Ltd, Harmondsworth, Middlesex, enclosing a cheque or postal order, and your name will be added to the mailing list.

Note: *Penguinews* and *Penguins in Print* are not available in the U.S.A. or Canada

GOGOL

Dead Souls

TRANSLATED BY DAVID MAGARSHACK

Gogol spent eight years writing the first part of *Dead
Souls*, which was published in 1842. Then his concep-
tion of the novel changed. In line with his mission to
save Russia he now saw it as an epic narrative in
three parts: the 'colossal figures' of his imagination
would uplift the Russian people and extricate them
from their predicament. He completed the second
part, but in despair destroyed it just before his death:
only fragments of it remain. Though his creative
dream was never realized, its superb gallery of
characters makes *Dead Souls* his greatest masterpiece.

THE PENGUIN CLASSICS

Some Recent Volumes